A Gentleman Bids for a Lady's Virtue . . .

Persephone found herself alone with Mr. Ramsey, a matter which she viewed with only moderate satisfaction.

"I never see you dance, Sir. Don't you enjoy it?"

"Why would I wish to dance when you do not?"

That was just the sort of thing Ramsey always *was* saying . . . "Surely there are others more worthy of your attention than I?"

He was staring at her in such a fixed manner that Persephone hardly knew where to look.

"Enough of this fencing, my dear. Neither of us is a child and both should know what we are about." And with that, and before Persephone could so much as say a word, Ramsey set out his offer to her in terms as explicit as they were generous . . .

Game of Hearts

Leonora Woodbury

CHARTER/DIAMOND BOOKS, NEW YORK

GAME OF HEARTS

A Charter/Diamond Book / published by arrangement with the author

PRINTING HISTORY
Charter/Diamond edition / September 1990

ISBN: 1-55773-388-0

Charter/Diamond Books are published by The Berkley Publishing Group, 200 Madison Avenue, New York, New York 10016.
The name "CHARTER/DIAMOND" and its logo are trademarks belonging to Charter Communications, Inc.

PRINTED IN THE UNITED STATES OF AMERICA

10 9 8 7 6 5 4 3 2 1

understatement. Even *crushing* barely captures the idea. *Grotesque* seems to me most appropriate, indicating at once, however weakly, their magnitude and my opinion of them and of my multitude of creditors. Haven't you anything left to sell?"

Persephone laughed, as she always did at Stephen's extravagant turns of phrase, but then responded with exasperation. "If you bothered to look around, you would realize my entire worldly store does not contain any item of nearly the value you seem to require. Indeed, I'd be hard pressed to raise one hundredth of such a princely sum, and let me tell you that if I could, I'd hardly be inclined to give it to you to pay off what I've no doubt are gaming debts. Or," she added as an afterthought, "to game again."

Indeed, the small and rather dingy drawing room in which the brother and sister sat gave mute testimony to the truth of Persephone's words. Aside from a few small touches such as a vase of fresh flowers and some handsomely embroidered pillows which reflected taste rather than wealth, the apartment was undeniably shabby. The hangings, once a deep French blue, had faded to an indeterminate gray; the rug might have come many years ago from Aubusson gleaming with vibrant colors but had long since paled to a dull dun; the furnishings, the gleanings of the last home which Persephone had shared with her brother and late father, bore the unmistakable signs of too many years of use with too few servants to maintain them.

Stephen, however, was unimpressed. "But that's just the point, Perse. Gaming's the only way I'll ever recruit our sadly fallen family fortunes, but unless I redeem the more pressing of my vowels, and that right quickly, I'll find the town notably thin of pigeons for my plucking. That is, of course, if I find the town at all, which ain't likely, since I'll either be arrested for debt by some

One

Persephone Welton looked at her brother in some bewilderment. She knew the young Lord Sandston to be volatile and guessed that he partook more copiously of what she had heard termed Blue Ruin than a fond sister would have desired, but she could not believe that he'd chosen to pay a morning call on his elder sister while in his cups. Still, it was difficult for her to believe that his alarming request had been made while sober. He knew her situation almost as well as she knew it herself, and it was not a good one. Widowed after only six months of marriage to a charming but impecunious line officer in His Majesty's army, she survived on the scanty remains of a very small inheritance left by her equally charming and even more impecunious father. She also had an uncanny ability to hunt out such bargains as were best calculated to give the appearance that her inheritance was sufficient to support not only life's necessities (which it scarcely was), but some of its luxuries as well (which it most certainly was not). Where, then, did Stephen expect her to get £1000?

"Perse, you know I wouldn't ask it if it weren't absolutely *vital* that I lay my hands on a very large cache of the ready. To call my debts *pressing* would be a gross tradesman or forced to go abroad to live down my dishonor."

"How can you speak so casually? As if I hadn't troubles enough. Are you really in danger of arrest?"

"But of course I am. I only wonder the same ain't true for you. How *do* you manage to maintain this show of respectability if you're as poor as you say you are?"

"By careful management and hard work, two qualities I dare say it has never crossed *your* mind to cultivate!"

"I should think not. Damned common sounding, if you ask me. Not virtues I expect to see in ladies and gentlemen of quality, let alone my own sister. Be pleased not to offend my delicate sensibilities by mentioning them again, or I may go off in a swoon. But this is taking us far afield. If you *can't* lend me the money, we shall have to come up with some other plan for getting it."

"We? *I* am not the one who seems not only unable to save so much as a brass farthing, but is too chuckleheaded to know that in gambling money follows money and that no one has *ever* recruited a family fortune without a sufficient stake to begin with, *nor* am I the one who has failed to notice that the Arringtons are all quite *fatally* unlucky at *all* games of chance. I am, however, the one who was busily darning a rent in my only really decent petticoat when interrupted by her fool of a brother!"

This speech, blighting in content and blistering in tone, appeared to affect Stephen only with mild amusement. "Now, Perse, don't take that tone. I can see your nerves are a little irritated, and I don't wonder at it if you've been going through the linen chest—I remember that always did make you low. But you know I'm a very *good* sort of card player, and in any event, that ain't the point. The point is that I need your help, and I know you'll not let me down."

That, of course, was entirely true. Stephen's volatility and recklessness had never stood in the way of his complete loyalty to his sister, nor of hers to him. The two had formed an alliance against the world almost since the time Stephen was old enough to toddle along behind his beautiful sister. That alliance was only cemented by the ensuing years, including as those years did the death of their mother and three still younger children in a single diphtheria epidemic followed by their father's increasingly erratic care.

Both recalled as if it had been yesterday the time that their fond parent had taken them to Bath and then, caught up in the excitement of a wager concerning how long it would take to ride a donkey to London, had forgotten them there. Stephen had been only ten years old, but had threatened to mill down the landlord of the hostelry where the two were left, their unpaid bill mounting by the day, should he attempt to carry out an eviction; but twelve-year-old Persephone had the more practical thought of applying for aid to Lady Winton, an old dragon, long established in Bath, who'd been a friend of their maternal grandmother. That redoubtable lady descended upon the landlord like an avenging angel and paid their shot. She had then placed them on the next stage to London with detailed instructions as to what Persephone should tell Lord Sandston of her opinion of him but the two children quite properly ignored these unfilial instructions.

They had returned to London none the worse for the experience, but increasingly convinced that their chief reliance must be on each other. Their father, to do him justice, had begun to wonder where they were, and could not have been happier to see them if they had been harbingers of the good luck he'd always felt was just beyond his grasp instead of the bearers of tidings of yet another debt. He was, in fact, genuinely fond of the two when he could be brought to remember their existence. He had congratulated his daughter on her sagacity in applying to old Lady Winton, who not only had been able to help when needed, but would almost certainly refuse to be repaid.

The passage of years, accompanied by heavy drinking and gambling and spent in the company of women to whom he could not introduce his children did not strengthen the bond between Lord Sandston and his progeny. Over the course of time, the two grew more distant from him and more close to each other, and their father's death brought little change to their lives. Nonetheless, Persephone's marriage to dashing Captain Welton had seemed at first likely to break up the brother and sister. David Welton was the most handsome creature Perse Arrington had ever seen and there was no doubt that he'd swept her off her feet, causing her to ignore the doubts which kept popping into her otherwise remarkably level head as to the wisdom of marrying the second son of the second son of an earl who was, himself, none too beforehand with the world. David's very charm of manner, so like that of her (moderately) lamented late Papa, should have warned her; so too should Stephen's surprising opposition to her marriage. Indeed, the very morning of the ceremony, Stephen had pulled her aside and shocked her by suggesting that it was still not too late to cry off. When she'd pointed out to him with some asperity that Captain Welton appeared to be just the sort of choice spirit the new Lord Sandston chose to favor with his company, Stephen had simply nodded owlishly and said, "Exactly." That Delphic pronouncement having done little to enlighten her as to the precise nature of Stephen's objections, Persephone had gone through with her wedding.

A few months of marriage managed to shed some light on Stephen's position. As David Welton's charm was ephemeral and largely reserved for those from whom he wanted something, little of it was expended on the wife who'd already gratified his desires by marrying him. Persephone had known when she married him that David lacked her interest in literature or art and found chess, her favorite diversion, to be a bore. What she had neither known nor expected was that he rapidly appeared to become equally bored by her company. While he seemed fond enough of his bride in a careless sort of way, that fondness was not strong enough to keep him home more than one night in ten, nor to keep him from squandering money at a pace which left Persephone, no novice at viewing the squandering of a fortune, dumbfounded. When one considered that a large portion of the money slipped from David's hands into those of bits of muslin who lacked even a tenth of his wife's beauty, intelligence or accomplishments, it was not remarkable that Persephone's temper began to veer toward the shrewish, but only that she managed to keep any control over it at all. Persephone had remarked bitterly to Stephen that he'd picked a fine time to become at once Gothic and discrete, warning her obliquely of Captain Welton's reputation without once telling her outright that he was a libertine and a spendthrift, but Stephen claimed that that sort of thing simply was Not Done, and Persephone had been forced to leave it at that.

Welton's scandalous death in a fight at the Cockpit Royal had seemed but his final assault on Persephone's peace of mind, although she was bound now to admit that she was well rid of him. Had he managed to leave her even a pittance, she might have even been ready to admit that he was simply a feckless creature, burdened by too much beauty and too little brain or character, more to be pitied than blamed. However, even her large tolerance for human frailty, after a lifetime of dealings with the more clever but no more responsible men of her own family, could not survive the information imparted to her by the solicitor who had served her family since her grandfather's day. Captain Welton had spent her entire dowry and sold what few heirloom jewels she'd brought to her marriage in order to support his gambling, and had left her with nothing more than a few hundred pounds and a few dozen trinkets, and little else except her fine family name and her beautiful face.

Where, then, was she to come up with any money to help Stephen? She was increasingly uncertain of her ability to help herself!

"There *is* Uncle Hezekiah," she suggested tentatively.

"What! Apply to that Bible-pounding, Methody-ridden, misbegotten changeling! Never!"

"Please, Stephen. That Bible-pounding, Methody-ridden, misbegotten changeling *nabob!* I can't say I like him any better than you, but it seems to me that it ill-behooves people in our position to condemn the only member of our family in five generations who has managed to gather more riches than he has wasted. I'm not saying I'd enjoy applying to him, nor yet that it is terribly likely that he will help us, but he *is* the closest thing to a chance we've got."

"Well that's where you're out. There's one way Aringtons have always managed to be provident, at least until you made such a cawker of yourself over David Welton. The only reason those five generations of Aringtons *had* any money to waste was that they always married more money than they had. If you can't give me cash, you're just going to have to help me marry an heiress."

"As if it were so simple. You're not the only man in London thinking the same thing, and heiresses aren't that easy to find. And what makes you think that *I* can be of any assistance?"

"You may think me chuckleheaded, although I must

say it was unkind of you to say so, but I ain't. I'm not talking about just *any* sort of heiress—I've a particular one in mind. You remember that tedious girl you went to school with, Rachel Thomason? You know, the one with the squint and the high-pitched voice?"

"Of course I remember Rachel. She did not squint, her voice was a pleasant soprano, and she had no more money than we did."

"And for all I know or care, she still don't. But what she does have is a cousin, and the cousin had a father, and the father had a cousin, and the cousin had a fortune, and the fortune had no place to go when the cousin and the father died together in a boating accident, and it turned out that it went to Rachel's cousin. And if you can't help me meet Rachel's cousin and make sure that fine fortune don't go a-begging, then you're not half the sister I think you are!"

"You know I don't go out into Society yet, and I haven't spoken to Rachel in years. I can't for the life of me see how I'm to arrange it, nor do I see much chance of its doing much good if I do. Surely, you're not the only man in London who has heard about this story."

"Well, so far as I can tell, they ain't been going out much as yet, so I doubt the girl's affections are engaged. You just arrange the introduction and make sure that she starts out with a good impression of me, and I'll handle the rest."

"Coxcomb. I'll give it some thought, but I'll have you know that I've as much faith in Uncle Hezekiah as I have in you."

Stating once again his opinion of their uncle and the chances of any good coming of applying to him, Stephen left his sister to her own thoughts. As Persephone combined a great deal of faith in Stephen's ability to charm anyone he chose with a near certainty that no guardian of an impressionable heiress would so much as consider allowing one to meet, let alone to marry, him, those thoughts turned largely on her uncle.

Any family tree as old and far-flung as that of the Arringtons was sure to bear an occasional odd fruit. Uncle Hezekiah was just such a one. Back in the early years of the reign of George III, Grandfather Arrington had lost a wife, the grandmother of Persephone and Stephen. Feeling the loss deeply, the old man had sought comfort in the company of a neighboring widow, a woman thirty years his junior, of some beauty, some brain, and copious religious fervor. An ardent follower of John Wesley, the widow had consented to marry her elderly swain on the condition that she be allowed to continue her abhorrence of Church and adherence to Chapel, and to raise any child of their union in her own religious beliefs. The besotted baron agreed, and the marriage took place to the signal consternation of Lord Sandston's chaplain and elder children. In the event, Uncle Hezekiah was the sole offspring of his parents, his father dying shortly after his birth. His mother, her convictions having only strengthened over time, followed her plan and reared her son strictly within the confines of her faith. The boy was raised with "The Blood of the Lamb" on his lips and a fervor for Godly industry in his heart, convinced of nothing so much as that God would reward his faithful in this world as well as the next, so long as the faithful were also honest, sober, hard-working, and capable of understanding the fundamental principles of lending at interest to sound business ventures.

Not surprisingly, young Hezekiah had little in common with or love for his half-brothers, the youngest of whom was fifteen years his senior, and the most solemn of whom considered the dinner wasted at which he did not breach his third bottle. When, following his mother's death, an opportunity appeared for Hezekiah to pursue his vocation for business in India, he leapt at it and disappeared from his country and from his family's thoughts for the next thirty years. Indeed, so thoroughly was Hezekiah estranged from the Arrington family that Persephone first heard his name mentioned when he arrived back in England shortly before her father's death; blackened, grizzled, fabulously wealthy, and apparently as little interested in his Church of England family as they had ever been in him.

Persephone's father had left his card; Persephone herself attempted a morning call. The card went unanswered; the call unappreciated. Uncle Hezekiah had taken one look at his niece and grunted "Jezebel," by which Persephone, though no Old Testament scholar, understood him to look upon her with something less than approval. As his next words were "Shut the door behind you on your way out," she felt justified in her initial impression, and had written her unexpected uncle off as a possible source of succor to her always-struggling family. She'd dutifully sent Uncle Hezekiah notes at the time of his brother's death, her own marriage, and her widowhood, but the only response she'd received was on the last occasion, when she'd opened a small package addressed to her in Hezekiah's crabbed fist and found a tract on Godly Widowhood. Feeling that this was of less comfort than she'd a right to expect from one who was, after all, not only a near relative but by all accounts as rich as Croesus, she'd thrown the pamphlet in the fire.

Now she wondered whether it had not perhaps been a hopeful sign that her uncle had bothered with even so minimal a gesture. Did he send tracts to *strange* widows? She thought not. Did the sending of a tract to her indicate the stirrings of at least *some* familial feeling? She hoped so. In any event, it now seemed well worth the effort to find out. While her first meeting with her uncle had not been propitious, he had consented to see her and had not actually had her physically ejected from the room. In her current state of mind, she chose to look on these facts as constituting little less than a rapturous welcome.

Yet even in her most optimistic state, Persephone was not so besotted as to believe that Stephen was likely to make anything but the worst of impressions on the old . . . dear. She might persuade him to comb his riotous black curls into something more sober than his normal Windswept style; she might urge him to adopt a less extravagant mode of tying his neckcloth than the elaborate Oriental he currently favored; she might even convince him to trade his delicate yellow pantaloons for a shade less likely to induce apoplexy in an aging Anglo-Indian Dissenter, but nothing could alter the wicked look in his eye or the Devil-may-care set of his mouth. Her own extraordinary looks were easier to tame—she looked equally beautiful with her auburn hair drawn back in a prim and Quakerish knot as with it dressed in luxuriant curls, and her creamy skin was as flattered by the blacks and grays of her half-mourning as it had been by the delicate pastels she'd worn during her come-out or the deep, jewel-like tones she'd favored during her brief marriage. More to the point, she'd learned over the years to adapt herself to the crotchets of those around her, and could trust herself to adopt an attitude that would, if anything could, incline her uncle to look favorably upon her as one who had suffered all the cruel disadvantages of a frivolous upbringing in a Church that was little better than Papist, but had, nonetheless, retained a core of solid virtues worthy of monetary reward.

Persephone set about, then, planning her attack on the stony citadel she envisioned as her Uncle Hezekiah's heart. She initially considered purchasing some Methodist works and committing enough of them to memory to pass herself off as a co-religionist, but rejected the plan both because her conscience would be bothered by the fraud and because such a deception, once adopted, would be difficult to shed. She didn't fancy the image of herself, throughout the coming years, busily attending Chapel and participating in Methodist sewing circles in return for some financial support from her uncle. Certainly, she was willing to present herself to him as bearing a more somber character than was literal truth, but she was unwilling to commit herself to a lifetime of sermons and sobriety.

Her thoughts having taken her this far, Persephone reached a decision. The time clearly had come to renew her approaches to her uncle. Retiring from the shabby drawing room to her even more dingy study (or so she called it; it was really a back parlor too small and dark to serve any useful function) she sat down at her writing desk, brushed aside the pile of unpaid bills lying on top of it, and composed what she flattered herself was a very artful note to Uncle Hezekiah. She thanked him for his thoughtful and uplifting gift at the time of her recent bereavement; apologized prettily for her laxity in responding to his gift, which she attributed to the shock of her sudden loss; and begged the honor of calling upon him so that she might, as she put it, heal a family breach which was none of her making and discover in what way she could be of assistance to her sole surviving uncle who had been too long away from his Native Shores. Next, she looked about for a pair of petit point bedroom slippers begun for her father during her schoolgirl days and put aside when that gentleman had pointed out quite kindly that he would not be seen dead in the items in question, intending to complete the slippers as a gift for her uncle. While she could not, upon reflection, fault her father's taste, she believed that Uncle Hezekiah might look kindly upon any gift from her own hands and, his fashion sense being an unknown, might even like the hideous things. As she could not in any case afford to purchase anything for her uncle commensurate with his enormous wealth, the slippers seemed a good gamble. She need never know if he consigned them to the nearest fire, and she hoped that he could not but be touched at such a very domestic sort of gift.

After finishing the note to Hezekiah, Persephone sat still for a few moments and then, considering that it could never do any harm to have more than one iron in the fire, she also undertook a second short note, this one to her old school friend Rachel Thomason. This missive, although perhaps equally artful, was more sincere than that which she wrote to her uncle, as she had a genuine fondness for Rachel. Though not perhaps quite so homely as one would have guessed from Stephen's strictures, Rachel was certainly no beauty, but she made up for lack of countenance and fortune with a great deal of good humor and good sense. While never one of Persephone's bosom bows, Rachel had been a good friend and had written to her upon the occasion of her father's death in a most touching way. Surprisingly, no similar letter had followed upon the published announcements either of Persephone's marriage or the death of her husband, but it was not impossible that Rachel had simply missed the news. Persephone knew her to spend much of the year in the wilds of Yorkshire visiting an elderly aunt from whom she had some expectations. Now, however, Persephone understood from Stephen that Rachel was living in London as a companion to her newly wealthy cousin. Persephone's letter to her was in the nature of a welcome back to London, in which she told Rachel of the changes in her own life and suggested that she might pay a morning call on her at Rachel's convenience. That completed, Persephone returned at last to darning her petticoat.

A letter came back from Rachel some days later indicating as Persephone had guessed that her friend had not had the least notion of her marriage or bereavement and expressing herself with such intelligent sympathy that Persephone found herself brushing away a few tears. The letter also invited Persephone to call whenever she wished, as Rachel and her cousin Hermione as yet knew few people in London and were rarely occupied during the day. Although still uncertain as to how renewing her acquaintanceship with Rachel could serve Stephen's purpose, Persephone resolved to pay her call as soon as possible, for her own sake, if not for Stephen's.

Two

As it fell out, it was only a few days after she heard from her friend that Persephone found herself in the neighborhood of the address which Stephen had given her as Rachel's. She had planned to spend the afternoon sitting with an elderly relative, a connection of her mother's who lived alone with her many cats and a companion in a small and unfashionable house in one of the more fashionable sections of London. Cousin Elvira was not only elderly but quite eccentric, not leaving the house more than a few times each year and seeing almost no one except her companion, her physician, a woman who came in once each week to tell her fortune from a deck of greasy playing cards, and Persephone, whom she never failed to abuse for having made a fool of herself over a pretty face. It was a tribute to Persephone's good nature that she continued to visit the old lady, coming at least once a month with a basket full of sweets which Elvira would not buy for herself, although she loved them and could better afford them than Persephone, and with such mild *on dits* as were likely pleasantly to scandalize.

On this occasion, though, it appeared that Persephone's good intentions were wasted. Elvira had determined on making one of her semi-annual forays into the shops of London, from which she would return with a collection of scarves, gloves, mittens, shawls, and turbans with which she would bedeck herself for the coming six months, to the secret amusement of Persephone and the loud scorn of Elvira's (even more eccentric) companion.

Wondering how she would spend the rest of the day, Persephone realized that she was but a short distance from the home of Mr. Peter Ramsey, the guardian of Stephen's heiress and the gentleman under whose protection both Rachel and her cousin were living. She decided, therefore, that this would be as good an opportunity as any to take up Rachel on her suggestion that Persephone should pay a call. A few minutes walk brought her to the house, but there, for the first time, Persephone hesitated. The style of the house was magnificent; its front an imposing wall of gleaming marble, with each window sparkling like a diamond. Persephone knew nothing personally of Mr. Ramsey (although the term "guardian" suggested to her a solemn gentleman, probably portly), but she was quite certain that the inhabitants of this impressive structure were not accustomed to receiving unattended females who arrived on foot and demanded to see one of the young ladies of the house. She wondered whether it might not be better to make a more formal call at a later date, spending some of her meager store of cash on a job carriage so that she could arrive in (borrowed) state.

No sooner had she decided to leave, though, than Persephone castigated herself for a coward. Poor she was, and poor she might appear to be, but she was *dashed* if she would turn tail simply at the sight of a large house, as if she had never been inside a fashionable residence in her life. Raising her head slightly higher, then, she marched up the broad stairs to the front door and lifted the massive knocker with a resolute hand. The crash with which the knocker announced her presence startled her, and her self-confidence was further eroded when the door was swung open by quite the haughtiest footman it had ever been her misfortune to encounter. His "Yes?" alone was enough nearly to freeze her blood, carrying with it an overtone which said not only "yes" but "Who are you and how dare you be knocking here?" Rather than making her excuses and running away, however, as was her immediate temptation, Persephone cleared her throat and asked in a tone which, had she but known it, she borrowed from her formidable former mama-in-law, for Miss Rachel Thomason. The footman inquired as to her name and, as she handed him a card, carefully folded at the corner, deigned to allow her into the house. He did not, however, ask her to wait in the drawing room, instead announcing that he would see whether Miss was in and whether she was receiving visitors. Persephone fumed at being left to cool her heels in the entryway, but amused herself by attempting to calculate exactly how many of her own small rooms would fit in the hall.

She'd barely begun her calculations when she heard a familiar voice from the top of the stairway. "How *dare* you leave Mrs. Welton waiting like that? Your master shall hear about this." And then, in a rush, Rachel was down the stairs, exclaiming, "Perse! How *do* you contrive to look even more beautiful than I remember, and that in widow's weeds? Come into the drawing room."

Rachel led the way into an apartment that was not only large, but light, airy, and furnished in the first style of elegance. She motioned her guest to be seated, and then turned to the haughty footman. "Joseph, please have tea brought to us immediately. Do you happen to know if Miss Pendergast is in the house?"

Joseph cleared his throat. "I believe that she is not,

Miss. She mentioned something about planning to walk about the neighborhood this afternoon."

Rachel made a face, and then asked, "Did she go out alone?"

"I believe that she did, Miss, her not having taken at all well to the suggestion that she might wish to have her maid with her, as she is, as yet, unfamiliar with London, and her maid not wishing to press the point." Here, Joseph paused. "If you understand my meaning, Miss."

"I understand you quite well, and would suggest that you go about your business at once!"

"Yes, Miss. Should Miss Pendergast come into the house, would you wish me to inform her that you are in the drawing room?"

"Please, and tell her that I have with me my old friend Persephone Welton, of whom she has heard me speak."

Joseph left the room, and Persephone looked an inquiry at Rachel. While she did not wish to appear vulgarly curious, there was no denying that Joseph's words and even more, his manner, had aroused her interest. Rachel laughed in a constrained fashion, and said, "You must know that my cousin was, perhaps, a bit spoiled in her youth. She was raised by her father after her mother died, and he did little to curb her"—Rachel paused for the *mot juste*—"exuberance." Then, suddenly, Rachel laughed aloud. "Oh, I don't know why I bother to give you words with the bark on—you'll discover the truth yourself soon enough. She's a vixen who did not hesitate to lock her last abigail in the closet when the girl suggested that Hermione's guardian might prefer that she not wander unaccompanied through London."

Persephone was surprised for a moment and then joined Rachel's laughter. "You poor darling. And here I was, turning nearly green with jealousy at your good fortune in having accompanied your cousin to London and acting as her companion in this beautiful house and instead, I find that you are almost as much to be pitied as I. Is it *too* awful?"

"No, I can't have you think that I am often the object of Hermione's bad temper. She considers me too poor a dab to waste her fire on, reserving much of that for her much-tried guardian whose house, you must know, this is. He is Mr. Peter Ramsey, and was Hermione's mother's eldest brother. No doubt you've heard of him—he's quite a notable sportsman, and I have reason to believe he knew your husband."

Persephone responded dryly. "My late husband knew so many notable sportsmen that I could scarcely keep track of them, particularly as he did not care to introduce me to many of them. Now that you tell me that, I do seem to recall the name, but am quite certain that I never met the gentleman." She laughed. "If he was a friend of Captain Welton, I must assume that he is a comparatively young man, and, if you'll pardon me, a comparatively"—she, too, seemed lost for the right word—"*high spirited* one. You must know that I'd imagined something quite different, though; while I was waiting for you I amused myself in drawing up a picture in my mind of the proper guardian for a young heiress, and I am quite sure that the guardian of my imagination had no fewer than fifty years in his plate and spent his evenings snoring over his Bible!"

Rachel smiled as well, and responded, "Well, Mr. Ramsey *did* say that he believed that he was not acquainted with you; I think you'll find your imagination did indeed lead you astray. And if you'll forgive me for saying it, he also said that while there was no man he'd rather have hunted with than David Welton, there was no one whom he would have less welcomed as a brother-in-law. Indeed, when I told him that you were likely to call, he suggested that I offer you his felicitations on your widowhood. As you can guess from that, he is a man with little concern for the proprieties, but my brief acquaintanceship with him has given me considerable respect for his judgment. Is it far afield in this case?"

"Not in the least. I'm surprised to hear the judgment of any of my late husband's particular friends commended, but it's as well that you've already heard something about Captain Welton, as I shouldn't like to mislead you and would be hard pressed to maintain the role of inconsolable widow for long. He was a handsome, good-tempered wastrel, and I've no doubt that if he had lived, he'd have had us in the workhouse by now. I cannot be glad he is dead—he was a young man, and not entirely without redeeming virtues—but I also cannot pretend that I don't regret having married him, for I most sincerely do."

"When I got your note, I wondered—had your marriage been a happy one I felt sure I'd have heard from you at the time it took place."

Persephone felt a stab of conscience at this, as she had to confess in all honesty that her failure to write to Rachel had arisen, not from unhappiness, but from her having put schoolfriend entirely out of her mind until reminded of her existence by Stephen. Still, it wouldn't do to dwell on that, and Persephone turned the conversation. "But my story is a common one—I made a foolish marriage and have lived to regret it. *Your* story is more in the nature of a fairy tale. How did it come about that you were chosen to accompany your delightful cousin to London, and to live in what appears to me to be truly *sinful* luxury in Mr. Ramsey's home?"

"That's easily explained. Hermione is five years my junior, and when we were both children had spent part of every summer with my family. Perhaps because I was older or perhaps because I was the only one who wouldn't stand her nonsense, I was and always have been the only person to whom she would pay the most mind. After she inherited her fortune her uncle, Mr. Ramsey, not only discovered that he had been named both her trustee and guardian, but was appalled to find that she was nearly a total savage; her father had so doted on her that he'd never permitted anyone to force her to learn *anything*. Mr. Ramsey, then, sent her off to a school in Bath for some polish, at least, if not for some education. She was asked to leave within the month—caught slipping out at night to attend a rout with a local sprig of fashion, I believe—and came here. As she is only sixteen, Mr. Ramsey thought to keep her in the schoolroom one more year and hired an extremely expensive governess to teach her at least some semblance of manners and a smattering of music. The woman left after two weeks, swearing that Hermione was possessed. Two elderly companions later, another relative of Hermione's remembered my ancient ability to exercise some control over her, and a letter was dispatched to my father begging that he would allow me to come to London to stay with Mr. Ramsey and his ward. We have not yet gone about much—I have convinced Hermione that she must at least learn some fundamentals of proper behavior before she is ready to be seen—but shall do so soon. *I* am getting out of this the London season my father could never have afforded, franked by Mr. Ramsey out of Hermione's fortune, and *he,* I hope, is getting at least some small peace of mind. I should add that Hermione no longer minds me as she was used to—as I said, she now thinks me rather a poor-spirited thing—but has formed the habit of believing me to know more than she does about how to go on in the world. Therefore, she is inclined to accept my advice as being in her own best interest, so long as it does not conflict *too* violently with her will."

"And you say that you are not to be pitied! It sounds horrid!"

"No, truly it is not. Hermione really does exercise her temper more on others than on me, and I would be less than human if I didn't enjoy buying clothes in the first stare of elegance and planning our attendance at all the most fashionable squeezes in London. Hermione's fortune and Mr. Ramsey's connections should gain us *entrée* everywhere, and so long as Hermione doesn't absolutely disgrace us all—something which is, I admit, a possibility—I shall rub along very well. For all of her temper, she's a lovely child, and is capable of behaving in a most winning manner at times. With her money and her face she is almost certain to go off in one Season, and I will retire once again to my quiet country life, broken only by my periodic attendance upon my great-aunt. I shall, however, at least have memories."

"Surely you haven't ignored the possibility that *you* may receive a offer during your Season?"

Rachel laughed. "Not ignored, no, but largely discounted. Come now, Perse, I wasn't a beauty when I was seventeen, and am surely even less of one now. Who is likely to offer for the plain and poverty-stricken companion to the Season's most taking heiress?"

"Some gentleman of sense!" Persephone responded severely. In fact, she was thinking that Rachel, while no more the beauty than she held herself out as being, had developed a great deal of countenance since she had seen her last, and privately believed that if Miss Pendergast were half the terror she sounded, some much put-upon gentleman might well find himself seeking comfort from her kind and sensible companion. That was, at least, what Persephone hoped, for she did not like the image of her friend retiring to the life of a spinster. She'd too much sense and character for that.

Tea had been brought and consumed some time before and as the two chatted, Persephone realized that it was growing quite late. As she had no wish to be caught out after dark, she was about to make her excuses when an upraised voice in the hall caught her attention. It was a deep voice, male, and at that moment, audibly irritable. Rachel exclaimed softly, "Oh, dear," as the voice was heard to say "And if you think that I shall allow you to attend any parties until I am convinced that you will not bring disgrace on your dead mother's name, you had best think again!"

A girl's voice, no less excited, answered, "Well, I *will* go to parties, and if you believe you can stop me, you will find that you are mistaken. I'll get what I want. You'll see. I always do."

The door to the drawing room then burst open and in rushed a dark and pretty young girl, dressed in the height of fashion (if not, perhaps, the best of taste), in a cerise velvet pelisse and high poke hat trimmed liberally with matching ribbons. She was obviously in the devil of a temper. "Rachel, love, *do* tell my *dearest* uncle that it is simply *Gothic* of him to fly into a pelter just because I found myself in the vicinity of St. James during my walk, and took the *least* peek at the Pall Mall. I did *not,* whatever ill-natured gossips may say, make a figure of myself by *parading* past the gentlemen in their clubs, and if Freddy Harris was kind enough to offer to drive me home in his curricle, *with* his groom behind us the whole way, so you needn't wonder otherwise, there is nothing to be said to it."

The girl was followed into the room by a gentleman, obviously laboring under a strong desire to wring his ward's neck. Peter Ramsey was approximately thirty-five years old and was very tall, well over six feet, and very dark. His face, while not handsome, had a great deal of strength and character to it, and his figure was slim and particularly good. At this moment, he did not appear to his greatest advantage, as he was visibly holding himself on a tight rein. Nonetheless, Persephone, viewing him surreptitiously but with some interest, concluded that he was decidedly attractive, if perhaps a bit masterful in appearance for her taste. Captain Welton's friends, she'd discovered after her marriage, generally were not so good-looking as he himself had been, most of them showing some signs of the dissipations in which they all routinely engaged. This, at least, could not be said of Peter Ramsey. He looked more the athlete than the rake.

"Miss Thomason," he began abruptly, and then stopped, noticing Persephone. "I'm sorry. I didn't know you had company. Perhaps when you've a moment free, you might grant me a brief interview. I should like to discuss what is to be done about this latest lapse in my niece's manners." With that, he turned on his heel, and left the room.

"Well, I like that!" Hermione exclaimed. "*He'll* discuss *my* manners. Why his own are notoriously the worst in London. I *didn't* do anything wrong, *did* I, dear?"

"It sounds to me like you most certainly did, goose, but I'll see what I can do later to calm Mr. Ramsey's temper. You really must not be flouting him like this all the time, Hermione. Little though you believe it, it is well within his power to ship you out of London and leave you to mope away the next two years in Sussex."

"Fiddle. He daren't. He knows that my father's brothers are just waiting for him to do something that they can tell Chancery is an abuse of trust so that *they* can be my trustees instead, and if he takes me away from London now, I'll surely run away and *then* think what a kick-up there'd be."

Persephone found herself gazing with a fascinated eye at this intrepid soul, wondering if the girl gave any thought at all to how her hoydenish ways would appear to the *ton,* or, indeed, to anything in the world except her own willfulness. In any event, the time was now long past that she should have left, and she started up, saying as she did so "I can see that you will be well occupied with family matters for some time now, Rachel, so I will take my leave. Please come to see me, when you can. There is much more I would like to talk to you about."

Rachel, too, stood, and gave Persephone a quick hug. She turned to her cousin and said "Hermione, this is my friend Persephone Welton. If you have not given her too marked a distaste for you with your outburst, perhaps she will have us both to tea sometime soon."

Hermione, never very interested in other women, nodded perfunctorily and murmured how happy she was to make Mrs. Welton's acquaintance and how she hoped to see her again soon. Persephone responded in kind, took a warmer farewell of Rachel, and went on her way.

Peter Ramsey, meanwhile, was in a fine, tearing rage. His guardianship of his niece was fair to driving him mad. He'd been genuinely fond of the girl's mother, his only sister, and though he'd only seen the child a few times after her mother's death, had been touched and pleased to find that he'd been named her guardian in her father's will. A few months' acquaintanceship with the chit had been enough to convince him that, far from feeling grateful to his late brother-in-law, he would have wished to resurrect him simply to slaughter him. The ward with whom he'd been saddled was, he was convinced, the most ignorant, ungoverned, ill-tempered, and ill-conditioned girl in the whole of England. He was a man who was accustomed to getting his own way, having been his own master since his father's death when he was only nineteen years old, and to find himself in continual strife with a child not yet quite seventeen years of age reduced him to speechless fury.

This latest incident was typical—not only had the

girl disobeyed his direct command that she not go out at all without some companion, but she'd flouted every convention by not simply walking about the streets, but by appearing where no lady should ever appear! And to top it all off, that Welton woman had chosen this day of all others to visit Rachel Thomason. He'd recognized the stunning creature in his drawing room immediately—he'd heard her described often enough by his friend Welton and had looked forward to meeting her when Rachel had mentioned her plan to call. While hardly a rake, Ramsey was not averse to female companionship and had, indeed, had some very prime articles in his keeping over the years. Based on his knowledge of David Welton and of both the late and current Lords Sandston, he expected to find Persephone to be a bit vulgar and probably more than a little mercenary, and would not necessarily have condemned either trait in her. He had a great deal to offer a moderately rapacious lightskirt, and if Persephone Welton combined those two traits with great beauty and a respectable name, so much the better. He had not expected, though, to make her acquaintance (or, more properly, to have failed to make her acquaintance) when he himself was showing to such particular disadvantage. He'd contemplated the possibility of some arrangement with the widow; he was annoyed that his first opportunity for commencing one had been spoiled by Hermione. If the occasion did not arise again, this would be yet one more offense against him by his infuriating niece.

Three

While Persephone waited, ever-hopeful, for some response from her Uncle Hezekiah, her life went on in much its accustomed way. Both her continued mourning period and her straitened financial condition forbade a very active social calendar, but the five years since her come-out were not enough to erase entirely from society's memory the most lovely debutante to have appeared in a dozen seasons, nor had various old schoolfriends, many of them now brides and mothers themselves, forgotten their good-humored companion. While she rarely went out, neither was Persephone often alone in the evening. Indeed, it was a rare night during which Simms, the ancient butler whom she'd inherited from her father because Stephen wouldn't have him and they couldn't afford to pension him off, did not open the door to at least a half-dozen souls who knew that her home was a place where one was almost certain to find congenial company and a roaring fire whenever nothing more formal presented itself. Not that Persephone could truly afford entertaining even on this modest scale and she frequently wondered just how much longer her wine merchant would allow her to run up a bill which he must realize there was little prospect of her ever paying. Still, she simply couldn't bear the idea of closing her doors to these casual visitors, nor of treating them shabbily once they were there. (Had she but known it, she was in no danger from her wine merchant. He was a sentimental young gentleman who had conceived a *tendre* for her years before when she'd been but a girl, turned loose by her father to compound with his creditors, and he was the promising heir to his father's business. Although his father was some years retired and he himself was now a happily married man, Mr. Williams remembered fondly the descents upon his shop of young Persephone Arrington and would no more have thought of troubling the beautiful widow with his bill than he would have his own wife. Her account was carried on a special page in his ledger, and carefully written off on a monthly basis.)

Persephone was aware that several of the men who had formed the habit of dropping in on her in the evenings were inclined to set up flirtations. None seemed to show any serious interest in her and, indeed, few could have afforded to marry one who came dowered with little more than a handsome Queen Anne desk, filled to the bursting with pressing debts; a wardrobe full of made-over dresses; and a knack for contriving. Thus, as she had no desire to become known as fast, she held these gentlemen at an unexceptionable distance and was careful to send on their way any such as had the misfortune to appear when none of her female friends were also about. She knew quite well that she should have a female companion living with her. However, she could not possibly afford either to feed some elderly relative (if one could be found who had not been so offended either by her father, her brother or her husband that she would be willing to live with Persephone) or to pay someone to fill the role of *duenna,* nor could she help but think that she would be unbearably chafed by such companionship. She had been raised almost exclusively in male company, and frequently found herself shockingly unable to enter into concerns which other females seemed to find fascinating. She chose, therefore, to believe that her widowhood was sufficient protection to her reputation and to maintain as much care of that reputation as she could by refusing to encourage any of her male friends in their efforts at dalliance.

She was enjoying a typical such evening at home only two nights after her meeting with Rachel, some few days after she'd sent her letter off to Uncle Hezekiah. Present were Lydia Fielding and Phoebe Barton, two young matrons whom she'd known since childhood, both currently deserted by spouses who had chosen to travel some distance to witness a mill which had promised more than usual excitement, as it was rumored that one of the fighters had previously killed a man with his fists.

Also in attendance were several military officers whom she'd met through her late husband, one accompanied by his very young wife, then in the late stages of "an interesting condition"; a gentleman laboring under the name of Herbert Hubert who had formed one of her court since her salad days; and Stephen, who'd arrived without notice in time to share her frugal evening meal (which he'd condemned as shabby) and stayed because, as he'd put it, "You appear currently to be the only person I know to whom I don't owe large sums of money, and having constantly to put off creditors does become rather *lowering,* don't you think?" She'd agreed heartily, only warning Stephen that her evening gatherings might be a bit slow for his taste, and begging that he not flirt too outrageously with Lydia since she was quite *fatally* susceptible to men with polished address, and her husband, for all his willingness to abandon his wife in London at the beginning of the Season, was not inclined to tolerate even the most innocent *cicisbeo.* Stephen agreed, and proceeded instead to devote himself to the blushing mother-to-be. He soon infected the entire company with his own high spirits. By ten o'clock, Stephen had organized a competition to suggest names for the baby and while some hostesses might have found the tone of the discussion a bit warm for their drawing room, Persephone was delighted to see everyone enjoying themselves so thoroughly. Herbert had just finished a lengthy and impassioned address on the iniquity of his parents in choosing for him the name with which his own father had been afflicted, when Persephone heard through the gales of laughter a knock on the front door. She was expecting no one else, and had long since sent poor Simms, who suffered badly from gout, to bed.

Stephen, still laughing, told Persephone to keep her seat and went off to find out who was calling on his sister at this unseasonable hour. She assumed that it was some friend who'd started the night elsewhere and found it dull, and looked quickly at the tray of light refreshments which sat on the sideboard to see whether there was enough for another guest.

She'd just begun to wonder why Stephen was so long and whether anything was amiss when the drawing-room door opened and he walked in. His expression was so odd that Persephone started up in consternation, and then saw over his shoulder that he was not alone. A few steps behind him were Uncle Hezekiah, looking exactly as he had the first time she met him except for a new pallor, and a homely young woman some few years Persephone's junior. The girl was sallow and very short, her plain features relieved only by a coil of glossy dark hair wound about her head, and luminous dark eyes. Before Persephone could take in much more than that, however, Stephen had audibly cleared his throat, and announced "Uncle Hezekiah and," humph, "Cousin Amelia."

Persephone blinked. What *was* Stephen talking about? She stepped forward awkwardly to greet her uncle, mentally cursing the ill-fortune which had led to their meeting again under circumstances which were unlikely to recommend her to him—entertaining select parties not being chief among the attributes of Godly widowhood, as she recalled—and looked inquiringly at the girl. Before she could formulate a question, though, her uncle spoke.

"Young jackanapes. Father was a jackanapes, too. So were all my brothers. I outlasted 'em all. Could have warned 'em I would. Clean living 'll tell. This is my daughter, Amelia. Just out from India. Mother was an Indian girl. Grandfather is a maharajah. She's his heir, and mine."

The silence which followed this speech, seeming to Persephone to last for hours as she racked her brain for some sort of response, was broken at last by Stephen, who drawled in his most affected tone, "How charmingly succinct! Can she play pianoforte as well?"

Persephone was ready to scream with vexation. Surely, this situation was one which called for some tact, and instead Stephen had chosen to be rude. She saw the color rise in Uncle Hezekiah's cheeks, and braced herself for an explosion, when she was amazed to hear a low chuckle from the direction of his daughter. The girl then spoke in a soft, somewhat deep, and attractive voice. "That will be quite enough, Papa. You've put my cousins and their guests to the blush, and I'll not have you make matters worse by flying into one of your rages. No, Cousin Stephen, I play no instrument, I sew no samplers, and I speak no languages but English and an Indian dialect that even few Indians understand. My father wishes me to marry, and I've no objection myself, but I do have certain doubts about the practicality of the scheme. And, as my father's announcement may have left some doubt in your mind, my mother *was* his wife."

Stephen burst out laughing. "Why, Cousin Amelia, how very *improper* of you! I can't help but feel that that is an excellent omen! You, and my uncle, of course, will sit down, I hope. As Perse seems to have forgotten her manners entirely, allow me to do the honors and offer you some ratafia."

Persephone, thus reminded that she was standing like a block in the middle of the room, her mouth agape while her new guests stood, shook her head as if to rid it of cobwebs, and summoned up a fair imitation of a welcoming smile. "Yes, Uncle. Do sit down, and let us get to know the new cousin you've brought us."

"Didn't expect to find company; widow still in weeds. Came to talk, not to drink. Still," Hezekiah added somewhat obscurely, "may serve my purpose. Tea."

Pausing only to wonder whether her uncle ever spoke in complete sentences, Persephone took this last remark to mean that Hezekiah would deign to take tea, and racked her brain as to how some was to be produced. None was ready; it was hours too late for tea drinking, and not only the elderly Simms but his youthful granddaughter who served as Persephone's scullery maid were long since a-bed. Nonetheless, Persephone assured her uncle that his tea would be along any moment, and went through the charade first of ringing for a tray, and then of furrowing her brow in mock irritation at the lack of a response. Stephen watched with some amusement, knowing full well that there wasn't a servant awake in the house, and nearly laughed aloud as Persephone exclaimed "How *can* I be so shatter-brained? You must know, Uncle, that my maid left Town this afternoon in the greatest haste, having just heard that her sister has been confined with her tenth child and her mother having chosen this inopportune time to contract a putrid sore throat." Casting a quelling glance at her brother who appeared to be choking, she went on, "Things are at such sixes and sevens that the tea tray was never made up. Will you take something else, perhaps?" And with that, she pointed beckoningly to the tray of refreshments. To her intense chagrin (and Stephen's unconcealed delight) her uncle responded, "Certainly; just thought tea would be easiest," and poured himself a brimming full glass of her only really good Madeira.

Meanwhile, the rest of her guests had rearranged themselves about the room. All were looking uncomfortable and she could see them formulating their excuses in their minds. This put her on her mettle; while she'd not necessarily have chosen for her uncle to join this particular company, neither was she about to slight her friends in his favor and so she set about exerting her considerable charm to restore some semblance of normality to the gathering. This proved somewhat easier than she'd expected, as it transpired that Uncle Hezekiah had, thirty-five years before, known the father of Mrs. Vanethorpe, the young bride, and was thoroughly taken up in detailing the more discreditable stories he could recall of that inoffensive gentleman. He therefore paid little attention to anyone else in the room, a circumstance for which all were profoundly grateful.

Amelia, having seen her father comfortably disposed in a large winged armchair, his Madeira and a digestive biscuit on the table at his side, seemed content to listen to the conversation near her, which came around, as such conversations inevitably do, to gossip about absent friends. Few comments were directed at her and as she knew none of the people being discussed, she could not have been expected to contribute. She did not seem uncomfortable, however, and the occasional remarks in her direction were turned off with a deprecating but not ungracious smile. Nonetheless, Persephone was not misled; it was obvious from Cousin Amelia's first remarks that she'd both a brain and a tongue in her head, and she was curious as to what the half-caste heiress was making of her first venture into English society. Her only clue came when her cousin said to her in a low voice that she was surprised to see the sobriety of the company as her father had given her to understand that strong liquors were commonly drunk in such circles as Persephone moved in. Persephone replied that that was certainly true at times, but that drunkenness was, perhaps, no longer quite so common as it had been when Hezekiah left England three decades before. She wondered, though, what other impressions the eccentric Methodist had given his daughter and whether the poor girl had any other sources of information about the society from which her father had fled. Of course, if Cousin Amelia shared her father's religious convictions, she was unlikely to wish to have much to do with society in any event, which would probably be just as well, given her color and her appearance. Still, she appeared pleasant and was at least a *half*-cousin and Persephone felt some sympathetic interest in her on that account alone. As to Uncle Hezekiah, the knowledge that he was not a lonely and solitary soul was something of a blow, but Persephone was a realist, and conceded to herself that she was unlikely to receive much aid from an uncle who had a daughter of his own to launch.

While Persephone was thus musing about the ruin of her not-very-substantial hopes, she heard her uncle turn to Stephen and ask him, in a surprisingly civil tone, whether cockfighting were still a popular pursuit among young men of fashion. When Stephen said that he believed it was but that he himself had little taste for it, Hezekiah snorted and commented dryly that he was, in that event, a different man from his father. Stephen agreed amiably that he was, indeed, not his father, and the conversation floundered there. Although she now believed that little could possibly come of it, Persephone could also see no harm in attempting to find favor for herself and Stephen with their uncle, and tried to pick up the conversational thread. "Uncle," she called out, "what have you found most changed since you first left England?"

"Petticoats; used to cover up everything; now, there's nothing you can't see, if you've a mind to look."

Mrs. Vanethorpe blushed a fiery red, as Stephen choked once again into his drink. Seeming not to notice the effect of his words, Hezekiah went on, "Petticoats, and bosoms. Used to be, all you could see was bosoms, and a sight too much of those. Nowadays, you see straight through those flimsy things that pass for gowns, with their waists up around their arms, and not a bit of honest fabric to be seen. Devil's work. Sodom and Gomorrah. More Madeira."

Persephone was at first uncertain as to how Madeira worked its way into this litany of sins, and then started up as she realized that her uncle was holding his glass out to her. Profoundly grateful for the first time for her heavy black skirts, she rose to offer more refreshments to all her guests. These had, however, universally concluded that a small dose of Hezekiah Arrington would last them quite well and each not only refused the offer of food and drink but remembered suddenly that they'd an engagement either later that evening or shockingly early the next morning. Each took leave of the Arringtons, father and daughter, civilly enough, but Mr. Hubert took the opportunity of murmuring in a low voice as he pressed Persephone's hand in a speaking manner that he doubted even the nabob's entire fortune would coax a suitor for her swarthy cousin. Persephone flushed in annoyance; the girl seemed well meaning and pleasant-spoken, and Persephone had no desire to participate in sport at her expense. She turned him off rather abruptly, then, but she couldn't help but wonder whether Mr. Hubert were not correct.

With the departure of her other guests, Persephone expected Uncle Hezekiah and Cousin Amelia to excuse themselves as well, leaving her to talk over this surprising turn of events with Stephen. The two, however, seemed in no hurry to go. Hezekiah nursed his Madeira, looking about him with a suspicious eye and hunched slightly over his glass as if he feared someone might attempt to snatch it from him, while his daughter sat peacefully, long since done with her own ratafia but seemingly content to take her lead from her father. Stephen cast a comical look of dismay at his sister, and exclaimed, "My—what a nice family party."

Amelia flushed at this, so slightly that Persephone was inclined to wonder whether she'd seen it at all, and Hezekiah gave a surprising crack of laughter.

"Cleverer than your father, too. That fool would just have told us outright to leave, and never would have known what it was that I wanted." As Stephen started to respond, he raised his hand, "Now, don't fly up in the boughs because I called your father a fool. Truth. But I'll admit that I liked him better than any of my father's other whelps. Wasn't vicious. Some of 'em were. Maybe that's why I've come to your sister—think I trust your father's children more than the rest and wouldn't mind doing you two a good turn at the same time. Not"—he seemed now to be musing to himself—"that the boy'll be of much use. Need a female; widow's better. But doubtless the boy can dance."

"Papa, there are four of us in the room, and you are talking to yourself. It's rude and confusing. If you want to talk to Cousin Persephone and to Cousin Stephen, talk to them, not in their general direction."

Persephone wondered if this was how Indian children characteristically addressed their parents, or whether her cousin Amelia was not, in her own way, as eccentric as Uncle Hezekiah himself. Certainly, neither her cousin nor her uncle seemed to find anything unusual in the fact that Amelia's attitude toward her father was strongly reminiscent of that of a tolerant governess toward a beloved but troublesome charge, and Persephone had to concede that it seemed to achieve its ends, for once again her uncle took his daughter's advice.

"Niece, I'll put it to you plain. My girl's no beauty, I know that, and she ain't just the right color, but she'll be one of the richest women in England some day, besides being as good a girl as any father could ever wish for. Says she's happy taking care of me, but it ain't what's right and I won't be around forever to need her caring. Want her to marry; want you to help. You bring Amelia out, and take her around to all the places she should go, and the day she marries, you'll have £10,000; even if she don't, if you play your part fair and square, I'll leave you five thousand in my will and I'll pay the freight for the Season. Pay up anything you owe now, too; can't have my daughter's chaperon arrested for debt."

Persephone was struck dumb by this proposal—an unlimited purse to draw on now and a promise of considerable monetary expectations whether her cousin married or not was largess beyond any she'd hoped for from her uncle in even her most sanguine dreams. Still, she found the proposition a bit odd and wondered why Amelia wasn't saying anything? She turned to the girl, and asked a bit uncertainly, "Do you *wish* me to chaperon you in London? Pardon me for asking, but certainly if you are a Methodist like your father, you may find the *ton* not at all to your liking." Here, she faltered, not certain as to how much more it would be proper to say. However, Amelia seemed to take no offense.

"As it happens, I am not a Methodist, much to my father's disappointment. My mother, you see, had been educated by an English governess, and was quite as devoted to the Church of England as my father is to his own faith, and my grandfather straightly forbad my being raised in any faith other than my mother's. Beyond that, I believe you would warn me that I may find my welcome something less than warm. I understand that; as I said at the first, I fear that my father's hopes for me may be impossible of achievement and that I may never marry. But I've an ambition to taste Society in any event, and it seems to me that viewing it with you will be great fun. I suspect there may be some reflected glory to being in the company of a great Beauty and that your circle of friends and acquaintances is likely to be an amusing one. If you are willing to play the *duenna* to your little foreign cousin, she would be most grateful; if you are not, she (and her father) will quite understand."

Feeling that this offer was a tide which it was, for some reason, necessary to resist, Persephone raised one last problem. "As you yourself pointed out, Uncle, I am not expected to go out into society as yet; my husband's death was less than one year ago. Of what use can I be now?"

"Thought about it. Husband was a wastrel. Cousin is new to the country. All right if you don't dance yourself."

Persephone had recently begun to wonder herself whether she might not start to go out again. The proprieties had been observed for some months, and her husband's treatment of her and the circumstances surrounding his death were sufficiently well known that prolonged mourning might simply be viewed as hypocritical, so there was little she could say to this. Stephen, too, added his agreement at this stage, pointing out that there were pale grays and lilacs of half-mourning which were quite appropriate to the ballroom, and that no one who knew Persephone could reasonably expect her to bury herself for years on end in tribute to a man such as Captain Welton. Protesting weakly that she was not talking about either burial or *years,* but only about one full year of formal mourning, Persephone asked her uncle if she might have a few days to think about his proposition. He agreed, adding only that she shouldn't waste too much time about it, as they were none of them getting any younger, and he and Amelia took their leave.

After seeing her guests out the door, Persephone returned to find Stephen staring thoughtfully into the fire.

"Well, Perse, I never thought that anything would come of your appeal to our uncle, but it seems I was wrong. Too bad that girl is so plain; she seems a nice enough little thing."

"You think I should accept his offer, then?"

"Lord, yes! Can there be any question? If you've £5000 to throw away, then you've been behaving damn shabbily, is all I have to say."

"Oh, you know very well I can use the money. It just seems, I don't know, somehow *dishonest,* as if I'm being paid for something I know I can't do."

"Come on now, Perse, you heard the girl. She has no illusions. She just wants you to let her see a bit of how Society goes on; *she* don't have any expectations, whatever our uncle may be thinking, and anyway, if she really has that much money, who's to say that someone may *not* marry her?"

"But that would be worse than anything! No one knows better than I the discomforts of marriage to a man who doesn't care a rap for you, and I can't help but think that Amelia would be better off remaining single than letting it be known that she's up for bid for anyone who wants a large fortune and doesn't care what he has to do to get it!"

"Well, but she's a big girl, and can take care of herself, or her father can take care of her. It's not *your* problem, my girl, nor need you think that every man who'd be thankful to marry a fortune would mistreat his wife in the bargain, thank you very much!"

"You know I didn't mean you—*you'll* not marry her, for all your fortune-hunting talk. You'll marry a beauty, or not at all."

"That's as may be; I shouldn't think I'd marry our cousin, in any case. But that's not the point. The point is that there's no need for you to be acting as if this stroke of quite *unprecedented* good fortune were some sort of trap. If you're not careful, you'll be turning Methody yourself, and *then* where will we all be?"

Laughing, Persephone answered that that would probably be the best way to cut Amelia out of her father's succession and then, as Stephen began to look alarmed, assured him that she would certainly consider her uncle's offer carefully and sent him on his way.

Retiring to her room, her head whirling, Persephone realized that her hesitation was rooted largely in a simple inability to believe that her luck had changed at last. After months of wracking her brain as to how to maintain even the simple life she now led, it seemed too good to be true that her debts could be paid and even a small fortune put aside simply for accompanying her cousin to exactly the sort of amusements she herself enjoyed. As she fell asleep, she thought that there was no question about accepting her uncle's offer; the only question was whether she would awaken in the morning to find the entire thing had been nothing but a dream.

Four

The next several weeks of Persephone's life were passed in a whirl of planning, choosing, fitting, and buying. *Modistes* who were formerly as far out of the reach of her slender purse as the moon was of her slim hands suddenly enjoyed the pleasure of outfitting a rare lady who combined the attributes of beauty, taste, and good temper. It was true that the requirements of her half-mourning limited these artists to more delicate shades, but as the lady looked lovely in lilacs and grays and as she was otherwise not averse to styles which were in the first kick of fashion, this restriction did little to spoil the dressmakers' enjoyment. The fact that they had at the same time to design gowns for the not nearly so lovely heiress was palliated by the fact that that lady was, if anything, even more free-spending than her cousin and was also, unique in the experience of London's more fashionable shops, equally good-humored. In fact, Madame Clarisse of Paris (born Clara Hopthorne of Chelsea, and unmarried) remarked to her chief assistant Mademoiselle Lisette (born Lila Hagstead, and the wife of a sea captain and mother of a promising brood of boys) that it was generally the case that there was a direct relation between how much money a girl had, how unattractive she was, and how irritable was her temper. Having fitted out some of the wealthiest girls to have appeared in London in recent years, she had considerable expertise on the question, and it was her opinion that she had never seen an heiress who matched Amelia Arrington either for homeliness or pleasant manner.

Persephone, however, found that Amelia's appearance seemed to improve the better one got to know her. Perhaps it was simply a matter of her expression which was generally serene and smiling, but it was also, she flattered herself, in part a matter of the excellent judgment which she, Persephone, showed in helping her cousin select her new wardrobe. Amelia herself was comparatively uninterested in fashion and had few opinions as to what she should or should not wear. Her father had always dressed her in sober colors which only emphasized her sallow complexion and lack of inches. Without wishing to turn the girl into a peacock, it was immediately apparent to Persephone that her cousin would look better in gay patterns, and she very much enjoyed choosing for Amelia the bright fabrics which she herself was still denied. She was particularly pleased when Amelia showed her some lengths of Indian silks which she had brought from her home, shyly suggesting that they might flatter Persephone. They were lovely things, but totally inappropriate for a widow. Held up against Amelia's dark skin, however, they seemed to take on a special glow and imparted their own light to her. Madame Clarisse no sooner saw them than she began planning the formal gowns which could be cut from their shining yards, and Persephone congratulated her cousin on having selected exactly the fabrics which showed her to best advantage.

The cousins' time was not spent just in shopping. While Persephone felt that they had to wait until some of the new gowns were ready before they could appear at any formal gatherings, she also realized that it was none too soon to begin to introduce Amelia in more casual settings nor to let it be known that she herself was emerging from her seclusion. She had always pitied young girls who were thrown too suddenly from the schoolroom into the ballroom. While that was not precisely Amelia's situation, Persephone did not want her cousin to find herself at her first crowded squeeze, knowing no one and the object of an undesirable amount of curiosity. As for herself, she continued to have some doubts about the propriety of abandoning her mourning before a full year was out but felt that it would appear less odd if she were to reintroduce herself into Society gradually.

As a result of these determinations, Persephone and Amelia began morning calls on numerous friends and acquaintances, some of whom she had not seen since before her marriage. She gratefully put off her black weeds for these calls, telling herself both that it was the best way to let people know that she was ready to receive invitations and that there was something particularly disheartening about appearing on someone's doorstep looking like nothing so much as an oversized crow. For these calls, she and Amelia had the use of the enormous town carriage that Uncle Hezekiah had commissioned as soon as he returned to London, and Persephone enjoyed that as well, telling herself that no footman was likely to look down his nose at ladies arriving in such state as that!

One of Persephone's first calls was to Peter Ramsey's house, and she took no small pleasure in asking Joseph, who once again opened the door to her, to step out and tell the coachman that, as both Miss Thomason and Miss Pendergast were in, it would be some time before he was needed again. She could not help but feel the difference between this call and her last one—now, wearing a dove gray gown with a lace flounce which alone cost more than all her widow's weeds together, arriving in a fine private carriage and secure in the knowledge that all her most pressing bills were paid and that there were real pound notes in her reticule. They were received once again in the magnificent drawing room which faced upon the Square, and Persephone was amused to find herself looking on the expensive furnishings (French, straw-colored satin, Thomas Gainsborough portraits) with a slightly condescending eye—Hezekiah's drawing room, in which *she* now entertained, was equally expensive (Chippendale and Sheraton, sky blue silk lustre, and Joshua Reynolds portraits) and she thought, in just slightly better taste.

Her visit to Rachel was almost entirely for her own pleasure; she was less inclined than ever to believe that anything would come of Stephen's plans concerning Rachel's young cousin, although she would have been hard pressed to explain exactly why. In plain fact, the chances of her arranging an introduction to the heiress were now considerably improved. The last time she had visited there seemed little probability that she would ever appear at any gathering at which the girl might be found, while now part of the reason for her visit was to let her friend know that her uncle was planning a small ball in his daughter's honor and to solicit Rachel's attendance, and Miss Pendergast's. Nonetheless, Persephone could not help but feel that lightning had struck the Arrington family once in the form of Uncle Hezekiah's surprising offer and was unlikely to strike again. She was inclined to think that Stephen's immediate problems would have to be solved out of her own pocket, and that some other idea would have to present itself for a long-lasting solution.

As Persephone had expected, Rachel and Amelia got along quite well from the first. In temperament, they were much alike, while it transpired that they also shared several interests, most notably in the poetry of various individuals of whom Persephone had not heard at all. They appeared to her untutored eye to be genuinely knowledgeable about poetical practices, and soon were engaged in a heated discussion of the role of the sonnet in modern writing. As Persephone had hoped that a friendship might form between the two, this was good; however, it left her at the mercy of Hermione Pendergast, an experience which she would readily have missed.

It appeared that Miss Pendergast was suffering all the irritations of a spoiled and petted Beauty subjected for the first time in her life to some discipline, and she was only too pleased to have a new audience before whom she could rehearse her grievances. Uncle Peter, it seemed, was not only a Tyrant and a Bully, but probably nursed Dark Designs on her Fortune. Indeed, it would not have surprised Hermione in the least if he wished entirely to *ruin* her social chances so that he could marry her off to some minion of his own and retain control over her vast wealth. As to how he planned to accomplish this ruin, Hermione was not entirely clear, although it was likely that an important aspect of it was his resolve to limit her forever to childish clothing and paltry jewelry which would make her appear not only infantile, but dowdy as well. (From this, Persephone correctly understood that Mr. Ramsey had quite properly refused to allow his ward to trick herself out like a piece of Haymarket ware and had informed her that she would not be allowed to wear the emerald and gold *parure* that formed a major part of her inherited collection until she was either married or old enough not to appear ridiculous in that imposing set.)

Rachel, having apparently heard at least some small part of this tirade, felt obliged to intervene. She first informed Hermione with some severity that ladies of fashion did not confide tedious family affairs to relative strangers, and then informed Persephone that she should pay no attention whatsoever to the silly girl's animadversions, as Mr. Ramsey was behaving in all ways most properly toward his ward. Persephone might have had her own ideas on that count, having taken good note of Mr. Ramsey's forceful appearance and obvious temper at their first meeting and having some secret sympathy for any young girl confined under his doubtless harsh authority, but she had intended to ignore Hermione's childish ramblings in any event. The warning, then, was unnecessary, but not surprisingly, Hermione took Rachel's statements in bad part and said with some dudgeon that it was easy for *her* to talk, as Uncle Peter always showed *her* the greatest respect and did not treat *her* like some sort of Moorish *slave* who had only to do exactly as she was told. She then announced peevishly that she had developed the headache and left the room.

Amelia had listened to all of this with her characteristic composure, and then turned to Rachel with a question. "Does the child simply lack manners or sense as well?"

Rachel raised an interrogative eyebrow, and Amelia laughed and gestured at the room about them. "I don't know the size of Miss Pendergast's inheritance, but if, as I understand it to be, this is Mr. Peter Ramsey's town house, that inheritance must be large, indeed, for it to weigh heavily with him. In fact, I believe I recognize the gentleman's name from some of my father's dealings. If it is the same man, I can't imagine that he is hanging out for anyone else's fortune; his own should be quite considerable."

Persephone and Rachel both looked down with some embarrassment, this frank discussion of money being not at all the thing. Amelia, noticing their constraint, said no more, and the rest of the visit passed unexceptionably, Persephone's invitation having been given and accepted by Rachel, with the proviso that their acceptance would have to be approved by Peter Ramsey. Rachel was able to assure Persephone, though, that that approval would almost certainly be forthcoming, as Mr. Ramsey had clearly despaired of his plan to keep his ward from any formal entertainments this year and a small affair given by an acquaintance of his own would probably be the best he could hope for her first appearance. The three had taken a fond farewell, and Persephone and her cousin departed.

In the carriage returning to Uncle Hezekiah's house, Persephone had ventured a hint to Amelia. "I believe that I know you too well, cousin, for you to take this amiss, and feel that it is part of my duty as *duenna* to warn you; it won't do for you to appear *too* conscious of the wealth of others, particularly given the rumors which I'm quite sure are already spreading like fire about how fabulously wealthy my uncle is. I'm sure I don't know why it is true, but it is certainly the case that while all Society knows that fortunes and their respective sizes are the subject of everyone's private attention, they are not often discussed in public."

Far from taking offense, Amelia had laughed. "I realized as soon as I'd made my remark about Mr. Ramsey that it had discommoded my hostess, and I *am* sorry for that. But I must say, I find English society rather odd in this respect. In India, money means neither more nor less than it seems to here in London, but the society in which I, at least, grew up, was much more honest about it. Marriages were generally made by families to consolidate fortunes, and exact gradations of wealth were a matter for much concern. Still, I do understand your point and will in the future attempt to appear as unconscious as you could wish, so long as you allow me to reserve to myself the right to make such private observations as occur to me."

Persephone readily agreed to that proposal, and perfect amity was restored.

The same could not be said of the situation at Peter Ramsey's house. As soon as Persephone and Amelia left, Hermione flew back into the sitting room. She hadn't taken much note of Persephone Welton when she had first seen her, being inclined to dismiss most women she met in any event, and certainly anyone clothed in a dowdy black gown which looked to have come from the hands of some third-rate seamstress with not an *ounce* of fashion about it. This time, however, she'd recognized in the older woman that most dangerous of creatures, a *Rival!* Modesty was not among Hermione's few virtues, and she knew herself to be an extremely pretty girl. Honesty, about others if not about herself, however, was a virtue to which she could lay claim, and she knew perfectly well that her beauty was a mere candle to the sun of Mrs. Welton's. The widow's very existence, then, was in some sort an affront to her, and she was not at all willing to add an actual humiliation to that. Had she been able to turn Mrs. Welton to her side in her battle with her uncle, she might have tolerated Rachel's friendship for the creature, but to be treated like a mere *child* in front of her was not to be borne!

She entered the room, then, with her chin tilted up and her pretty face flushed, and had burst out to Rachel "How *dare* you humiliate me in front of That Woman that way? Couldn't you see her *laughing* at me? I shall *never* forgive you."

Rachel, well used to her cousin's tantrums, kept her temper. "Don't be ridiculous. Persephone Welton has seen too much of the world to bother laughing at you. If there was any humiliation, which there was not, you brought it on yourself with your ungoverned tongue. You know I've warned you that your attitude toward your uncle is not only improper but will have the most *off* appearance to Society and, really, if you cannot be trusted to control yourself any better, I shall have to withdraw our acceptance of Mrs. Welton's kind invitation."

Hermione had left the room before any discussion of the ball, and this caught her attention as Rachel had known it would.

"What invitation?"

No sooner had Rachel explained the purpose of Persephone and Amelia's visit than Hermione forgot all her temper. "A *ball!* My first real London *ball!* I shall need a dress. I shall need a *dozen* dresses, just so that I can pick the *perfect* one. And I'll need flowers, and jewels, and Uncle Peter *must* let me wear the emeralds *now.*"

It was most unfortunate that Mr. Ramsey chose just that moment to enter the room, for he heard the tail end of this speech, and without waiting for any explanation, said grimly "Oh no, Uncle Peter shall not. And if Uncle Peter hears one more word about those blasted emeralds (which are not only too sophisticated for you, but quite hideous as well), I shall have the things tossed into the Thames!"

Always ready to rise to any bait, Hermione had shot back "Then I *shall* be able to have you removed as my trustee, for I *know* that *must* be a breach of trust."

Hastily intervening before Mr. Ramsey completely forgot himself and took his infuriating niece over his knee then and there, as was beginning to seem likely, Rachel interjected, "Don't be ridiculous, Hermione. You hardly want to worry about a suit in Chancery when you have just been invited to your first real London ball."

"What ball?"

"Oh, Uncle Peter. It's the most *wonderful* thing, and so long as you let me go, I shan't be angry with you at all, or even plague you about my emeralds, even though they *are* mine and I *should* wear them and they're *not* hideous and . . ."

"What ball?"

"Really, sir, you can't blame your niece for being excited. It truly is the most wonderful thing. My friend Persephone Welton was just here with her cousin, Amelia Arrington, and they've invited us to a ball which Amelia's father is giving in honor of her arrival in London. Do please say that we may go; I feel sure that it will be just the sort of gathering which would be right for Miss Pendergast's first appearance, and I should dearly love it myself."

"Persephone Welton is Hezekiah Arrington's niece? Why I'll be"—he paused—"dashed. I'd always assumed Sandston was some sort of collateral relative of Hezekiah's—there doesn't seem to be much family likeness." And he laughed. Rachel, not knowing Hezekiah Arrington, had no idea what amused him, but was pleased to see that his mood had softened. "Then we may go?"

"Oh, yes. Certainly. I'll not keep my niece from any party of Hezekiah Arrington's." And, still laughing, he walked out the door. So Persephone Welton was old Hezekiah's niece? That complicated things somewhat. Hezekiah Arrington was not only an old friend of Peter Ramsey's from the period Ramsey had spent in India some years earlier, learning the fundamentals of the Indian trade, but was also a valued business associate. He'd known that Mrs. Welton's maiden name had been Arrington, but had thought (if he gave it any thought at all) that the relationship must be a very distant one. Seducing Hezekiah's niece might pose some problems. Still, this invitation was fortuitous in several respects—he would make sure that Rachel understood that Hermione would not make her bow to Society without his presence, so he would have an opportunity to see Mrs. Welton again and under more favorable circumstances for dalliance than their first meeting. And he would be able to observe the relationship between Hezekiah and his unlikely niece; if, as seemed probable, Hezekiah had no use for The Welton, he could proceed with his own plans with little to hinder him. In the less probable event that they seemed, well, *familial,* he might be forced to reconsider. Still, it promised an amusing evening.

Meanwhile, plans for Amelia's ball proceeded apace. In Persephone's opinion, it would be best to launch Amelia with a small affair, both to allow her to find her feet and to minimize the opportunity for the ill-natured to imply that she was attempting to buy her way into the *ton* with a tastelessly large debut. Nonetheless, she found that her own list of friends and acquaintances who might well be insulted at being omitted was large enough that it was reasonable to expect that no fewer than two hundred people would be in attendance. Invitations had dutifully gone out to Rachel and Miss Pendergast and included Mr. Ramsey as well. Persephone had been uncertain as to whether Mr. Ramsey should receive an invitation, as she had never properly been introduced to him, but the day after their call, she received a note from Rachel indicating delicately that the gentleman would be grateful to be invited to what looked to be his ward's first formal appearance. Stephen, as might be expected, was less than grateful for this consideration on Persephone's part, remarking when told of it that if he had known that she would plan to place obstacles in the way of his making up to the girl, he never would have sought her help in the first place.

Persephone had warned Stephen that Miss Pendergast was a pretty little child with the temper of an archwife and as little broke to the saddle as an unbridled colt. He'd merely remarked that he had never objected to a bit of life in his female companions, and as he'd seemed prepared to expound on this theme in a series of most improper reminiscences about some of the ladies he'd had under his protection since he'd first left Oxford, she'd ended the conversation there. She seriously hoped, however, that Stephen would abandon his planned pursuit of the girl, as she was convinced that what appeared merely as a slightly comical tendency to be headstrong in a sixteen-year-old girl was likely to turn into a quite intolerable shrewishness in a mature woman. Despite the girl's fortune, Persephone could not think of a female she had met in many years whom she would less like to see as her sister-in-law. However, as there was little she could do about the matter, and less likelihood that anything would come of it, she attempted to put the question out of her mind.

That was easy to do, as there were innumerable details to be taken care of before the ball, and no one but herself with the slightest idea of how to go about the preparations. The experience of ordering food, champagne, decorations, and music without any thought to expense was a heady one; even such trivial details as informing the Watch that there would be a crush of carriages on their street on the night in question was enjoyable. Persephone's only prior experience with the Watch had been the memorable occasion upon which several members of that organization had carried her father home, Lord Sandston having drunk enough to be unable to navigate the streets himself, but not so much that he was unable to exercise his considerable charm on those notoriously unsympathetic public servants. Their attitude at that time had been surprisingly friendly, even paternal, toward her, but it did not compare with the respect she was shown on *this* occasion.

Similarly, her pleasure at being able to place a large order with the patient Mr. Williams, and paying in cash at the same time, was unalloyed. (She would have been much amused to discover that her prompt payment of Mr. Williams's bill upon her recent accession to wealth had been a great disappointment to that gentleman.)

Her decision to fill the room with hothouse flowers was greeted with much enthusiasm by Amelia, who confessed that the profusion of blossoms was one of the things she most missed from her Indian home, while when Madame Clarisse delivered their gowns for a final fitting a few days before the ball, Persephone could not but congratulate herself on her insistence that Amelia appear dressed in her own silks; skillfully cut by Madame Clarisse herself in such a manner as to appear to add inches to Amelia's small figure, the shimmering colors emphasized her luxuriant hair and dark eyes, and made her look almost attractive. Persephone's own gown was also a success, and even Uncle Hezekiah commented that the two girls looked to do him proud.

Persephone had seen relatively little of Uncle Hezekiah during her weeks under his roof. It appeared that, far from having retired from business, he was still very actively involved and went into the City every morning, coming home only just in time for the evening meal. Aside from his insistence that the house strictly observe the Sabbath, only stirring to attend services (he, to his Chapel; she and Amelia, to St. George's, Hanover Square) and neither allowing them to pay calls nor to receive visitors, and his habit of reading some verses of the Old Testament aloud to them before retiring on most nights, she was unable to see any particular signs of his religion in his everyday life. Nor could she discern any particular interest on his part as to how his plans for his daughter were progressing. Still, it did appear to her that he was genuinely fond of Amelia, pleased when she spent time with him and glad to see her enjoying herself. Persephone had been a bit concerned as to what he would think about the more daring of the gowns she'd had commissioned for Amelia, fearing that they might stretch his tolerance too far, but aside from commenting that he didn't understand why girls should want to hobble themselves with those straight skirts, he'd made few comments on their new wardrobes. Indeed, when he was shown Amelia's ball dress, he had positively smiled, and said that she reminded him of her mother.

After that comment, Persephone had ventured to ask Amelia about her mother and her mother's family, about whom she had quite a burning curiosity. It appeared that Amelia's grandfather was not really, as Uncle Hezekiah had claimed, a maharajah, which Amelia explained to Persephone was a sort of a prince. Had he been one, and she his heir, she could hardly have left the country with her father. Instead, he was an extremely wealthy merchant who had had dealings with Hezekiah over the years, and to whom he had introduced his only daughter when she was merely fifteen and Hezekiah already a successful man in his middle thirties. Amelia's memories of her mother were rather vague, that lady having died when Amelia was only six years old, but her impression from what was said to her by her grandfather and by her own governess had always been that her parents had been a devoted couple despite their differences in age, upbringing, culture, and religion. Religion had, indeed, been perhaps the only point of tension between Hezekiah and his bride, but on that point the wife had been successful.

When Amelia had achieved the age of nineteen without receiving a single proposal of marriage from any eligible suitor (she had, she said, received several from young men who were grossly unacceptable, either to her because of their characters, or to her father or grandfather because of their lack of fortune), the two men had decided that it was time to give her a chance in her father's homeland. It was thus that Persephone learned that her uncle did not necessarily plan to remain in England once his goal had been achieved, but hoped to return to India within the year. In India, he was regarded as a leader of the Dissenting community;

there was much to draw him back there, and little to keep him in England. Surprisingly, then, Amelia *did* hope to remain in England, should she in fact marry. While she was quite reticent about this, Persephone had the distinct impression that as fond as Amelia was of both her father and her grandfather, a lifetime of dealing with two strong-willed old men had convinced her that their influence could be felt quite well enough at a distance of several thousand miles, and that the availability of an excellent mail service would adequately ameliorate the sorrows of prolonged separations.

In any event, Persephone was pleased to discover that this was the trend of Amelia's thoughts, as she felt it extremely unlikely that any of the men to whom Amelia was about to be introduced would choose to remove to India, and did not pursue the matter any further. Time was passing, and there were still dozens of important tasks as well as minor details to take care of before the ball.

Five

The first and most pressing of Persephone's tasks was to send out invitations based upon the list which she had so carefully drawn up of those who must, and those who might, be invited to her cousin's come-out. In so doing, she received a terrible shock. Uncle Hezekiah, it seemed, was not certain whether he would choose to honor them with his presence. Since it hadn't occurred to Persephone that there could be any question on this vital matter, she broached it with him only on the day the invitations were ready to go out. She ventured into her uncle's study that evening, something she rarely did, as it was understood that Hezekiah relished a bit of time to himself at the end of the day. She found him ensconced in a large winged chair, perusing a volume of sermons from an American minister of whom she had heard vaguely at one time, a Cotton Mather. She understood the Reverend Mather not only to have been dead for more than a century but also to have been no Methodist, but a Puritan, and was surprised at that choice of reading matter. Upon inquiry, she was interested to find that her uncle read extensively of all manner of religious writings, finding comparisons between other sects and his own Methodism informative. She'd not thought her uncle of having an inquiring mind, and felt that she had, perhaps, misjudged him. He, in turn, was obviously pleasantly surprised to find that his niece had so much as heard of either the Reverend Mather or his Puritans. What he said, in point of fact, was "Hmph! Not so empty-headed as I thought. Should have realized *someone* in your family had to have a brain to keep things together. Wasn't your father. Shouldn't guess it was your brother. No one else *but* you to keep 'em from ending in the workhouse. But you didn't come in here for compliments, nor to find out what I choose to read in the evenings. Well?"

"Well, Uncle, as we are preparing to launch my cousin, I wondered whether there were any of your old acquaintances (or new ones, for that matter) whom you wish invited to the ball. I should hope that there will be some of your companions there, so that you don't find the evening too dreary."

"Why should I? I won't be there."

"Not be there? But, Uncle, you can't have considered what an odd appearance that will have. Surely, you plan to welcome your own guests to your own home?"

"Not my guests. Yours and Amelia's. None of *my* friends want anything to do with your balls, and your dancing, and your frills and furbelows. Ha! See *me* tricked out like some sort of Bond Street Beau. Not likely. Won't happen. Won't do it."

Persephone was torn between laughter and annoyance. "We are hardly speaking of tricking you out like anything at all but the mature and respectable gentleman that you are!"

"Make me sound like an antique. Fifty-five."

Refusing to be diverted by this unexpected display of vanity, Persephone simply went on. "Uncle, I can't believe that you are serious. I understand that you yourself may choose not to dance; indeed, no one would expect it of you. And certainly I had no thought that you would join your guests in drinking, or in playing at cards. Indeed, I have meant to ask whether you've any objection to some whist tables being set out in the small drawing room for some of the older guests, but I had never thought that you might refuse entirely to attend your own daughter's ball. Who, pray tell, did you intend to act as your host?"

"Don't need a host. Amelia's always been the hostess in my home, and you two can greet the guests."

"Really, Uncle Hezekiah, you've not been gone from England so long that you remember nothing about how we go on here. When did you ever attend a ball without a host?"

"Never attended balls. Attended Chapel. Don't want to start with balls now."

For some time, Persephone was unable to shake him from that position. It was only Amelia's assurance to her that her father would come around in the end, if they gave him time and didn't worry him to death, that allowed Persephone to send out the invitations at all, as she knew very well that the ball could not go forward if her uncle continued in his refusal to grace it. However, events proved once again that Amelia knew her father well. Two days before the ball, they had received hundreds of notes accepting their kind invitation and matters were well under way for an evening which would be at least memorable, and perhaps brilliant. Hezekiah's continued silence as to his intentions was Persephone's sole concern, and her heart leapt to her throat when, shortly before they were to dine only forty-eight hours before the party was set to begin, she was requested by her uncle's cadaverous valet to attend that gentleman in his bedchamber at her convenience. When she arrived there a few minutes later, she found that her uncle had had laid out a somewhat somber but extremely tasteful suit of clothes for a gentleman of fashion planning to attend a formal ball. She paused in the doorway, and her uncle threw at her over his shoulder "Occurred to me that some of the old cats might think I was ashamed of my girl. Will this do?"

Stammering that the suit would do admirably, Persephone made her excuses and fled to her own room to give some more thought to the perplexing problem of her uncle's character. The suit had obviously been ordered some weeks earlier; no tailor could have taken her uncle's measurements and made it up in less time. Obviously, then, her uncle's comments to her had not been serious. Obviously, too, he'd a shrewd head on his shoulders. His statement about Amelia was one which she had thought, but feared to say to him. The conclusion to her ruminations was that she must be careful to remember that her uncle, despite his oddities, was no fool, for all that his abrupt and sometimes comical speech could mislead one.

The day of the ball arrived at last. It was neither delayed by the fact that the provisions from Guntners were inexplicably late and did not appear at the house until well into the afternoon, nor sped by the fact that Persephone and Amelia (as well, no doubt, as some dozens of other pleasure-loving ladies) could scarcely contain their excitement any longer. Contrary to Persephone's secret expectations, time followed its normal course, the sun rose and set, and it was time to dress her hair in the Grecian knot she favored for formal occasions and to don her ball gown, a stunning creation in lilac and pearl gray with a demure neckline and a graceful semi-train.

When at last Persephone, Amelia, Stephen, and Hezekiah had gathered in the dining room some hours before the ball was to begin, she thought again what an unexpected man her uncle was. While no more handsome than his daughter was beautiful, he looked sufficiently dignified in his new clothes that Persephone was able to draw a secret sigh of relief that he would not disgrace either his daughter or himself, at least so long as he did not choose to display loudly or publicly any of his more odd humors. Even as to that concern, she was reassured by his mild treatment of Stephen, whom she privately believed to provide as strict a test of his uncle's temper as it would undergo that night.

In the weeks since Persephone had moved to the Arrington establishment, Stephen had been a frequent visitor, and it could not be said that he and Hezekiah had precisely warmed to each other. It had not taken Hezekiah long to discover that a significant portion of the generous pocket money which he provided to Persephone was going to her brother, and while he had told *her* that the money was hers to waste as she chose, he had told Stephen that there was a name for men who lived off women, but that it was not one which he would care to repeat. Stephen had flushed deeply at the rebuke, and then laughed it off with the comment that he would not have expected his uncle to liken his payments to Persephone to immoral earnings, a response which hardly eased the situation. It had, once again, only been Amelia's intervention which saved them all from a very noisy scene.

On the occasion of Amelia's coming-out ball, however, Stephen was apparently determined to make himself agreeable. Things began well when, for a wonder, he arrived no more than a half hour after the time his sister had given him. Knowing her brother of old, Persephone had set that time at least forty-five minutes before that which Uncle Hezekiah had decreed for their dinner, and it appeared to their uncle that his lordship had in fact arrived somewhat early, an occurrence which predisposed him in his favor. Further, Persephone had warned Stephen that to arrive dressed in the most extreme of fashions, as was his wont, would be unlikely to endear him either to their uncle or, more to the point, to Mr. Peter Ramsey. Stephen had taken that sisterly advice to heart. His suit, though not quite so sober as Hezekiah's, was by no means outlandish, and Persephone could have sworn that Stephen had both put his coat on himself and was able (with some effort) to turn his head in spite of his neckcloth. As these feats were normally quite beyond his capabilities, this marked a considerable improvement. Finally, Stephen arrived at the house remarkably sober, confiding to Persephone that he'd had nothing more to drink that day than an ale with his breakfast at eleven o'clock and a slight restorative just before coming to strengthen him for the ordeal of dinner with the nabob.

Uncle Hezekiah seemed similarly determined to avoid any unseemly brawls with his nephew. When Lord Sandston was announced, he'd looked up keenly, but seemed reasonably pleased with what he saw, announcing, "Look less like a man-milliner than usual. Good thing. Like your shoes."

As Stephen looked down with some surprise at the items which had excited his uncle's admiration (black pumps for dancing, and by no means unusual), Hezekiah went on "You'll open the ball with Amelia. Dances well. Hope you do, too. In any event, it will look well for both of you: *she's* part of the Arrington family; *you're* in my good graces. Should save you a few points at the next cent per cent you go to."

"Thank you, Uncle, very considerate indeed. And I can think of nothing I would enjoy more than to dance with my cousin."

Persephone was pleased to see that this latter comment was made with a graceful bow to Amelia and with none of the sarcasm which she might have feared. Indeed, when she thought about it, Amelia and Stephen seemed to get on quite well, Amelia having quickly adopted toward Stephen much of Persephone's own tone, and Stephen responding well to this sisterly treatment. They all went down to dinner together, Persephone on Hezekiah's arm and Amelia on Stephen's, and enjoyed the excellent repast served up by Uncle Hezekiah's outrageously overpaid French cook. Hezekiah ate sparingly, as was his habit, and did not take any wine but seemed to enjoy the modest meal he made and showed all signs of continuing good spirits. Persephone had been a little concerned about Amelia, wondering how her nerves would deal with what was, for some girls, a shattering experience, but realized quickly that Amelia was, as usual, serene. Of course, her situation was not exactly that of a girl freshly out of the schoolroom; as Hezekiah had pointed out, Amelia had acted as his hostess in India for some years. The assurance which those years had given her stood her now in good stead.

As their guests began to arrive, to be greeted at the top of the stairs by Hezekiah and Amelia, Persephone noted with approval that her cousin's inherent grace did not desert her. Looking nearly handsome in her glowing gown, her hair coiled in lustrous plaits about her head and simple but stunning (and, as Persephone knew, stunningly expensive) pearls adorning her ears, throat, and wrists, Amelia's manner was exactly what Persephone would have wished, at once assured but unassertive.

Rachel, her cousin, and Mr. Ramsey were among the first guests to arrive. To Amelia's surprise, Mr. Ramsey was greeted by her father as a old friend. Her surprise was even greater when he turned to her and said, bowing over her hand, "I believe that I should claim the rights of an uncle of sorts; you are certain not to remember, but I gave you sweets when you were little more than a baby, and you thanked me by being sick in my lap."

Amelia turned to her father in some confusion, and he laughed. "True. But ungallant to remember. Came to India as a lad. Worked in my House. Good head for business. None for women."

A crack of laughter was surprised out of Ramsey. "I suppose I can't accuse *you* of being ungallant, Hezekiah, but would have you spare my blushes. Your father," he said, turning back to Amelia, "suffers from that most unforgivable of virtues, a good memory. But I can see we have you thoroughly bewildered, which is indeed ungallant at your debut. I spent several years in India when I was little more than a lad, and your parents both were very kind to me. Indeed, how your mother put up with me, I will never know, for I was a singularly foolish young person, and I believe I confided more tales of woe to her than could be found in a dozen tragedies. She was a remarkable woman, although only a few years my senior. I was devastated to hear of her death after I returned to England. You have probably been told this before, but you are very like her."

Amelia had, in fact, been told very little about her mother, her father not being of the sort to confide in his daughter, and her grandfather still feeling his daughter's loss too deeply to wish to speak greatly of her. She was pleased, then, to find that there was someone in England who had actually known her, and would have asked more had not her duties as hostess constrained her to turn to the new guests who were entering the room. As it was, she simply smiled at Mr. Ramsey.

Watching from across the room, Persephone found her first impression of Mr. Ramsey confirmed; while hardly an Adonis, Ramsey was a very attractive man, if somewhat saturnine in appearance. He did look as if he would be more at home in the hunting field than he was in the ballroom, but Persephone was not put off by that and Ramsey wore his inches with an athlete's grace. When he spoke with Amelia, about what

Persephone could not guess, his expression softened somewhat, and he looked positively handsome.

Rachel was dressed simply in a gown almost as discrete in shade as Persephone's own, and would have looked quite well had it not been for an expression of worry that was unmistakable to her old friend. The reason for the worry was not hard to find; Miss Pendergast, overdressed in a white gown trimmed with layer upon layer of Alençon lace, was in all-too-apparent high spirits. Her pretty face was flushed from the first moment they appeared and even from a distance, Persephone could hear her laughing, too high, too loudly, and too frequently. She'd noticed that while Uncle Hezekiah had seemed pleased to see Ramsey's party when they first came in, his face had darkened with annoyance at something Miss Pendergast said as Mr. Ramsey was turning away, and shuddered to think what it might have been. Stephen, who had been nearby, was able to enlighten her later both as to Ramsey's conversation with Amelia and Hermione's with Hezekiah. Upon being introduced to Hezekiah, Hermione had dropped a schoolgirl curtsy and then giggled, "I've heard of *you!* You're a Methodist, and rich as Midas. Don't you have *rules* against giving balls? Shall the Pope do something *awful* to you?" She was hurried away by Rachel before Hezekiah could respond, but Mr. Ramsey had managed to soothe him somewhat by saying, "I beg you will forgive my niece, Sir. You may find it hard to believe, but Miss Pendergast is only ignorant, and not ill-meaning. If you wish, I'll endeavor to take her home, but as I wouldn't bet a groat on my being able to do so without bringing on a fit of high hysterics, I hope you won't require it. Please accept my apologies for her as if she had the good grace or sense to make them herself." Hezekiah had grunted and let the matter go at that.

Persephone herself hurried across the room to greet

Rachel (as well as Miss Pendergast and Mr. Ramsey), and reached them at almost the same time as Stephen, who was bowing over Rachel's hand and claiming the privilege of old acquaintance. As she arrived, she heard Stephen say, "But I remember you *quite* clearly, I assure you. You visited Perse one summer holiday, and the two of you followed me when I went fishing, made loud noises to frighten the fish, and ended by falling into the stream in a successful but thoroughly unnecessary effort to warn the fish that I was there and nourished fell designs upon them. Perse then exercised the prerogatives of an elder sister and made me run home to find you blankets so that you shouldn't freeze to death, and compelled me to proceed you to the house so that you could sneak in without being seen by the governess."

"You're right, of course; it's not a day that I will ever forget, I believe. But how you recognized me, I can't guess. I will be horribly frank and confess that I should never have known *you.* All *I* recall was a dark, skinny little boy, and surely *I* still had my hair in pigtails, and was covered in freckles?"

The honest answer to Rachel's question was that Stephen would not have known her from Eve, and had only recognized the threesome of Rachel, Hermione, and Peter Ramsey from Persephone's descriptions, but he was hardly about to admit that. Instead, he'd laughed and protested that he had never been so *very* skinny, and that as he considered her the first distressed damsel it had ever been his honor to rescue, her countenance was imprinted forever on his memory.

Mr. Ramsey, cynically aware that his niece was much more likely the true object of Lord Sandston's regard than her companion, would have made short work of sending him about his business had he not realized that Stephen's presence at Hermione's side was likely to attract The Welton to his own. Thus, instead of the blighting set down he would otherwise have given, Ramsey greeted Stephen cordially, asking a casual question about a horse they'd both considered at Tattersalls some weeks earlier, and continuing the conversation until Persephone and Rachel had had a few moments to exchange greetings. He then addressed himself to Persephone. "Mrs. Welton, I hope you will grant me the same indulgence which Miss Thomason has shown your brother and allow me to greet you as if we were old acquaintances. I was shockingly rude when you were at my home visiting Miss Thomason and my ward, and as I have wished, in any case, to extend my condolences to you, I would like the opportunity to do so now. As I believe you know, I was well acquainted with your late husband."

Persephone was unsure how to take this speech. It could well be intended as a none-too-subtle reproach for throwing off her mourning so soon, but as she remembered Rachel's comments about Mr. Ramsey's view of her late husband, she thought that was unlikely. Deciding not to read too much into what was probably a casual remark, she simply inclined her head and murmured her thanks. It seemed, however, that more was expected. "Welton was not, I would be forced to say, always the most *steady* companion, but in some matters he is sadly missed; I never knew his like for judging either a horse or a woman."

Persephone blushed slightly. The compliment was a bit fulsome for her taste, but was delivered with enough grace that she could not take offense and, in any event, it appeared that the man was an acquaintance and business associate of her uncle and hence entitled to some measure of her good opinion. Instead of a mild set down, then, which she would otherwise have given, she smiled slightly, but could not forbear to respond, "I will take that as a compliment, sir, but would point out that Captain Welton's taste in horses, while undoubtedly sound, was occasionally led astray by his preference for rather showy beasts."

"He showed more discernment, I'm sure, in other matters."

Again, Persephone smiled, although now in a slightly distracted way. Mr. Ramsey's ballroom manners were much what she would have expected from a friend of David Welton's, but there was no denying that a light flirtation with a personable gentleman was a pleasant enough way to begin a ball for a lady who had attended none in some time. Still, she had other duties to perform and guests to whom to attend. She replied, then, that as an informal hostess of the gathering, she could not spend her entire evening with any one party of guests, however agreeable, made her excuses, and walked away. She saw that Stephen remained, and was not surprised when he told her a few minutes later that he had obtained Rachel's hand for the first quadrille, and Hermione's for the first waltz.

Ramsey watched Persephone walk away with a satisfied expression on his face. He'd made his first cast, and was pleased with the result. Hezekiah Arrington had made no special effort to greet his niece, which argued at least a possible indifference. As to The Welton, her manners were good enough; even ladylike. But he believed he saw through them to the flirt underneath. That she'd accepted his compliments with pleasure was obvious; that she'd accept more than that as the game progressed was likely. A woman such as The Welton, with a family and a name, was not to be approached exactly as one did a bit of muslin, with a simple and straightforward proposition of exchange. Some sort of wooing was expected, if only to present a more respectable face to the world. The result was the same, but the process was a bit more lengthy and delicate. Such delicacy, though, didn't disturb Peter Ramsey. It was, itself, a part of the diversion, not unlike the first steps in a dance. Opening bows having been exchanged, the next steps should, he thought, follow a predictable pattern.

All unaware that she was engaged in what Mr. Ramsey believed to be a *metaphorical* dance, Persephone had meanwhile steeled herself to resist the temptations of *actual* dance. She'd given the matter some thought, and decided that to disport herself on the dance floor might be considered by some people outside of enough for a widow still in half-mourning. Nonetheless, she found that she was quickly surrounded by gentlemen who were all too anxious to dance or, once they understood that to be out of the question, to flirt, to bring her glasses of negus, and in general to pay all too much attention to her and all too little to the many eligible young girls who were scattered about the room, obviously longing to dance and trying hard not to show their envy of the beautiful widow.

Persephone would have been more than human had she not enjoyed the attention that she was receiving after what seemed like years of neglect. However, she was also conscious of her duties, and steadily turned off her various admirers, skillfully introducing them to the young ladies in need of partners and carefully keeping an eye on Amelia at all times to be certain that she was not allowed to hug the wall at her own party. Persephone was gratified to see that Amelia needed none of her assistance; while hardly as thronged as she herself was, Amelia also seemed never to lack a partner, and was, in fact, dancing with all of the most eligible men in the room. Persephone cornered Stephen at one point, anxious to hear what sort of opinion the men had of Amelia and was pleased to discover that she appeared to be taking surprisingly well. According to Stephen, the consensus was that there had been many *homelier* heiresses foisted upon Society in recent years, and that her pleasant manner and enormous wealth were considered to be adequate compensation for her unfortunate complexion. Stephen himself reported that he had found Amelia to be a most satisfactory dancing partner. She moved gracefully, and knew her steps well enough that she was not forced, as so many girls were at their come-out, to concentrate all her attention on her own feet. Persephone, who'd spent many a weary hour with her cousin teaching her various dances, felt some pride at this, and indeed, at the way the whole evening was progressing. Her one source of concern was Stephen. Much to her chagrin, he seemed to be quite taken with little Hermione, telling her that the girl was refreshingly forthright. Thinking back upon some of the heiress's more outrageous comments, she remarked that she took him to mean by that that the girl had shared with him some thoroughly improper confidence which no lady of taste or sense would think of entrusting to a stranger. Stephen had grinned and replied that she obviously knew the child well, and didn't she think that Miss Pendergast's readiness to share with him what would have seemed to be the most intimate details of her situation showed a charming *naïveté?* Snapping back that it did not, she had flounced away in high dudgeon. She couldn't believe that Stephen was serious, nor did she like to think that he really might be prepared to become entangled with the difficult heiress.

It was also apparent that she was not the only person at the ball who did not look with approval upon Stephen's pursuit. She noticed Mr. Ramsey watching the two as they glided about the room in their *second* waltz and was not in the least surprised to see Mr. Ramsey pull his ward aside when the dance was finished, obviously attempting to draw her attention to the fact that she would be ill-advised to make so obvious a show of her favor as to dance yet again with Lord Sandston. As it was equally apparent that the girl was paying him no mind whatsoever, but instead arguing and, finally, turning up her pert little nose and walking away, Persephone was prepared when she was approached shortly thereafter by Mr. Ramsey himself.

Peter Ramsey was, not for the first time, contemplating murdering his niece. Ever since the formal invitation for the Arringtons' ball had arrived she'd done nothing but plague him until he felt sure that he would go mad. First there had been the matter of her gown. Despite her comments to Rachel, Hermione understood quite well that she could not buy more than one gown for the ball; even with her large fortune, her uncle would not permit her such needless extravagance. She was determined, then, that the gown she purchased should be absolutely *perfect.* Unfortunately, Hermione had been raised in relative seclusion from fashionable life by an adoring father who almost entirely lacked either taste, sense, or judgment as to appropriate female garb. The result was that Hermione's taste was, put simply, execrable. Left to her own devices, Hermione's gown would be garish, over-trimmed, cut too low in the bodice, and probably of a cloth so fine as to be nearly invisible. Ramsey, while not pretending to enormous fashion acumen, had enough sense to know that if his niece were to appear in a gown of her own choosing, social ostracism would be the likely result. Not surprisingly, however, convincing Hermione of this was a difficult task and he'd had to endure countless scenes, tantrums, and alarums in order to get Hermione to the ball even in the somewhat vulgar, but at least modest, gown in which she finally appeared.

After the matter of the gown was settled, battle was joined over what jewels Hermione would be permitted to wear. The emeralds were resurrected no fewer than a dozen times; when Hermione was brought to understand that she simply would not be permitted to wear those, she asked instead for diamonds. She'd settled for rubies, but only after more interminable scenes.

As for attempting to give the child any idea of the behavior that would be expected of her at her first appearance in Society, he and Rachel might as well have tried to instruct a wild animal! Every suggestion was greeted either with laughter or a saucy reply, while her last comment before entering the carriage on their way to the Arringtons' was that they needn't think that she was going to spend her time simpering in the corner and curtsying to old biddies, because she was *not.*

In his more sanguine moments, he'd imagined that once he got his niece launched into Society with a few careful introductions and a word to Rachel, the Arrington ball would be a tedious affair relieved only by an *a suivie* flirtation with the widow. Convinced by their first conversation that her virtue was assailable, he'd hoped that a few moments of private observation of Hezekiah with his niece at the first opportunity would tell him whether he should make the attempt. He quickly discovered, however, that the task of launching Hermione, far from being tedious, was filled with intense activity as he was continually tracking her down to the most private corners of the house so as to wrench her away from ardent beaux. When at last he found himself in conversation with the Beauty, his temper was considerably inflamed and his plans for dalliance were largely forgotten. All he really wanted was a chance to relieve some of his ill-humor.

"Pardon me, ma'am, but Miss Thomason has told me that you are a woman of excellent sense, and are somewhat familiar with the troubles I have encountered with my ward. As she appears entirely oblivious to the impression she is likely to make if she allows your brother to sit in her pocket at this, her first public appearance, I would beg your indulgence and ask whether you might hint your brother off. You might tell him that not only is my ward's fortune tied up until the age of twenty-five should she marry without my consent, but that she shows every sign of being one of those tiresome chits who is forever imagining herself in love, and will almost certainly become weary of him as quickly as she did of her dancing master, the young man with whom she attempted to run off in Bath, and the half-dozen other youths to whom she has repeatedly attempted to plight her troth."

Had Mr. Ramsey made his appeal in somewhat different terms, Persephone would have been inclined to sympathy even though she would also have felt obliged in all honesty to inform him that there was little she could say which would be likely to influence her brother in this. However, both Ramsey's words and his tone offended her. That she was aware of Stephen's mercenary plans was one thing; for this *person* to imply that Stephen was little better than a vulgar fortune hunter was unacceptable. Thus, Persephone answered coldly, "I can't imagine of what interest you think all of that information should be to my brother, who is only being kind to a child who should still be in the schoolroom. However, I will certainly suggest to Lord Sandston that there are other young ladies here more worthy of his attention than a girl who has not even the manners to make some show of obedience to her guardian, however poorly that guardian may exert his authority."

"*Touché!* You remind me that my lack of control over the girl is my own problem, not yours. I agree." He appeared to brood for a moment, and then gave a rueful grin. "And I can't for the life of me think why I should be wasting my time and yours on such a hopelessly tedious topic as my ward. For if you were to convince your brother to abandon his pursuit of her, I should simply find myself addressing the same speech to some other father, mother, sister, or guardian. As

I say, I believe my ward to be an incorrigible flirt and if you could persuade Sandston to behave with more propriety, she would simply abandon him in favor of someone who would behave with less."

This speech, delivered as it was in a self-mocking tone, did much to mollify Persephone; that was, indeed, its intent. Ramsey had not failed to note the widow's apparent outrage at the aspersions cast at her brother, and it served to remind him that Captain Welton had frequently complained (when in his cups and seeking to justify his inattention to his new bride) that Lord Sandston was in fact the only person for whom his wife truly cared. Recognizing that criticizing Stephen's behavior toward Hermione to The Welton could only irritate her while serving little purpose—after all, she would probably delight in seeing him ensnare the heiress—he'd come to his senses just in time. He'd think of some other way to queer Sandston's pitch; for now, he'd his own interests to think of. Seeing that the widow still looked annoyed, he'd smiled again. "Surely we can think of something more congenial to speak of than my infuriating niece. This is, I believe, your first appearance since coming out of mourning. Do you find the *ton* much changed?"

Persephone was of two minds. On the one hand, she was still annoyed at Ramsey for his impertinence. On the other, she was also annoyed at Stephen for behaving in such a manner as to justify Ramsey's suspicions, and was, in addition, inclined rather to like the man. She could see little point in cutting him, in any event; as she hoped to maintain her friendship with Rachel Thomason, she was likely to see more of him than would be comfortable if they were quarrelling. Her answer, then, was civil enough. "Do you know, I don't, and I am much surprised. I have several times this evening been told what I was promised was the latest *on dit,* only to find that it is the very story I heard at my *last* ball, only concerning different individuals!"

Ramsey laughed. "You would say, then, that scandal is never new?"

"Or, as my uncle is fond of reminding us, that *nothing* is ever new."

Ramsey intoned, in a reasonable imitation of Hezekiah's manner when reading Scriptures, " 'Vanity of vanities . . .' "

And Persephone finished, " 'all is vanity; and there is nothing new under the sun.' "

"I take it that Mr. Arrington is still fond of Ecclesiastes. He read it aloud regularly in the evenings when I resided with him in India."

"And still does to this day. I would not find it so lowering, I believe, if he did not look at me in the most *meaning* way while doing it. My cousin assures me that it is nothing but my uncle's nearsightedness, but it always appears to me that he is looking directly into my innermost soul, and not finding much to his liking!"

At this juncture, Ramsey noticed that his niece had once again disappeared from the ballroom and felt reluctantly compelled to excuse himself. He was satisfied with the progress he was making, and convinced that the woman's comments contained a subtle encouragement to him to try his hand further. (Persephone, in the meanwhile, all unaware of the construction Mr. Ramsey had given her words, was pleased as well. The ball was a success, her cousin appeared to be happy, and she herself had made the acquaintance of a seemingly unexceptionable gentleman. She must, she scolded herself, get over her irrational prejudice against any man who had so much as known Captain Welton!)

Persephone did not see any member of the Ramsey party again that evening, although she looked forward to seeing them at numerous engagements which were to begin soon, as the Season got properly underway.

In tribute to Mr. Ramsey's pleasant behavior to herself, though, and much against her will, she had found herself echoing his words about Miss Pendergast to Stephen.

"Stephen, setting to one side the fact that you are taking shameless advantage of the girl's innocence to encourage her to behave in such a fashion that she will likely be denied admittance to half the houses in Mayfair, it's my belief that you are wasting your time. Not only is she an obvious flirt but it is my understanding that her fortune will not be her own until she is twenty-five if she marries without her guardian's consent. You can hardly think that encouraging her to make a figure of herself is the best way to win that consent, if it is to be won by you at all, which I heartily doubt."

Stephen's reply struck dismay in her heart. "I've warned you, Perse, that your poverty has tended to make you terribly *common* in recent months. How *can* you think only of money when you see that charming creature? I assure you most earnestly that *I* do not." As she began to protest, he held up his hand. "Oh, I know that when I asked you to arrange for me to meet her I had only the most *mercenary* of motives; doubtless, this will be some kind of lesson to me, though I cannot for the moment imagine what. But I'd no idea how delightful a child she would turn out to be. I know I've heard you speak slightingly of her temper, but really, how much of that is simply reaction to her beast of an uncle? *I,* for one, credit him with all of her excesses; what spirited girl would not be led to kicking up some larks when that Sunday-faced shabster is pinching at her all the time? Why, he even begrudges her any but paltry trinkets, when anyone can see that a girl like that *has* to have pretty things about her."

Hearing Hermione's own ill-founded complaints thus repeated by her brother, Persephone rose to Mr. Ramsey's defense, and in an effort to bring her brother back to some semblance of reality, felt constrained to point out that the delicate ruby *parure* which the girl was wearing could not have cost a penny less than £400, and as such could hardly be called paltry; she herself would dearly love to possess such a "trinket." As this only led to Stephen pointing out that Mr. Ramsey could hardly allow his ward to go about looking positively *shabby,* Persephone might just as well have spared her breath. She found it hard to believe that Stephen was really as taken with Miss Pendergast as he said, but whether his feeling was genuine or simply a game, she could not tell. The worry that it was genuine, however, was enough to cloud her enjoyment of the evening.

Aside from her worries about Stephen, though, the evening contained many matters for satisfaction. Chief among them was the reception that her cousin Amelia received. There could be no doubt that Stephen's description of the reaction to their cousin was fundamentally correct; she had definitely *taken.* That her hand was besought for every dance was not, perhaps, surprising; the ball was in her honor, and there were enough gentlemen of breeding in the room who would have felt obliged to rescue her from hugging the walls that Persephone had expected her cousin to enjoy at least a reasonable amount of attention. But there was no question that there were many gentlemen at the ball who sought Amelia's hand not out of politeness, but out of a desire to enjoy her company. When she chose not to dance, several budding young swains disputed for the privilege of bringing her negus, and when she expressed a desire for some air, no fewer than five offered their arm for a stroll to the conservatory. Persephone credited Amelia's successes both to her appearance, considerably improved as it was by careful dressing, and to her character, and thought somewhat the better of London's gentlemen for their apparent appreciation. She'd not have been surprised to hear that the talk in the clubs the next day was more of Amelia's fortune than her charms, but would have been relieved to find that the tenor of the commentary was friendly, and the thrust of the discussion was largely what a relief it was to find an heiress with whom it was not a burden to stand up. Her color was the subject of some unkind comment, but less than might have been expected; it was generally felt that she was not so very plain as rumour had led the gentlemen to fear.

Another surprising source of pleasure was her uncle. Despite her victory in bringing Hezekiah up to scratch and into the ballroom, Persephone had cherished no very high hopes for his flattering any of the guests with his attention. However, she found that she had misjudged the man; having agreed to come to the ball for his daughter's sake, he was obviously determined not to run shy and harm her chances by making a figure of himself. As Persephone had noted from the start, he looked surprisingly well and carried himself with a great deal of dignity, if some reserve. He was too long unaccustomed to this sort of event to carry it off entirely comfortably—several times Persephone had found herself in his vicinity, and endured his muttered comments on their guests, including a scandalized exclamation, "Paint! That hussy is wearing paint!", but as far as she could determine, he confined these strictures largely to himself. At one point she noticed him in conversation with Mr. Ramsey, and once with Rachel, an event which both surprised and pleased her. Meeting Rachel a few minutes later, she asked what she and her uncle had talked about, and found that Rachel's family were near neighbors to some old cronies of Hezekiah's, about whom he had inquired. In fact, although Rachel did not report it fully to Persephone, her conversation with Mr. Arrington had amused Rachel considerably.

Rachel had come to the ball expecting to spend most of her time attempting to restrain her cousin, but she had soon given up the effort. Hermione's parting words in the carriage had made no less of an impression upon Rachel than upon Mr. Ramsey, while Rachel's first comment to her young cousin about the unwisdom of giving the old cats something to talk about had been received with a flounce and a shrug of the girl's shoulder. As Hermione had gone from her straight to Stephen Arrington, against whom she had been specifically warned, Rachel decided that attempts to control the girl would simply drive her to greater excesses. She had determined, then, to let nature take its course. When she'd informed Mr. Ramsey of her decision, he'd grimaced and said that while he believed that she was probably right, he did feel obliged at least to make the attempt to exercise some control, although he could not tell her how he planned to achieve that laudable goal. In any event, feeling herself absolved from responsibility for the heiress, Rachel had settled back to enjoy herself. As she'd expected, few of the young men who so eagerly surrounded her cousin paid the least attention to her older, less attractive, and less wealthy companion, but that bothered her little. She was a mediocre dancer and was considerably more interested in observing the crowd than in being observed. That pastime proved, indeed, an amusing one, and when she'd found herself near her host at one point, she was unable to resist exclaiming, "This is the best of good fun, Sir! You can't think how grateful I (and my cousin, of course) are for your having us to your ball. Why, just looking at the crowd is like"—Rachel paused, searching for the right word, and Mr. Arrington triumphantly completed her sentence—"visiting Bartholomew Fair!"

Rachel choked off a laugh, and responded, "How unjust you are to the Fair, Sir. I'm sure *it* can boast *consid-*

erably odder sights than this, although I will confess that I doubt it can do any better than *match* that gentleman for comic effect." The unfortunate youth to whom Rachel drew Hezekiah's attention was an obvious member of the dandy set, and thought himself complete to a shade, the shade, in this case, being the palest primrose, a color which repeated itself not only in his pantaloons and coat but also, and most daringly, in his dance pumps. He felt that this fashion *coup,* should it catch on, would make his name as well known as Brummel's had been in his day, and believed most sincerely that only a philistine could fail to be struck by his ingenuity.

Mr. Arrington responded with an unexpected grin. "My niece is forever trying to convince me that this precious *ton* of hers is not near so outlandish as I remember. Gives me less respect for her judgment than I'd like, if she thinks *that* ain't outlandish."

"I assure you, Sir, that Perse would share our feelings entirely. Indeed, I believe that you cannot value her good sense highly enough. So many beauties lack either judgment or delicacy; even when we were schoolgirls together, she was most notable for both."

"Like the girl. She likes you. You, Amelia, Persephone—good chits."

Not knowing how to respond to this unforseen praise, Rachel had turned the conversation to common acquaintances before making her excuses. She parted from the old gentleman some minutes later on the best of terms, thinking that he was not entirely lacking in the notorious Arrington charm even if his manner of exerting it was a trifle eccentric.

Hermione's pleasure in the ball was unalloyed. She'd discovered quickly after coming to live with her uncle that she possessed a powerful weapon against him. He had some concern for what others thought of him; she genuinely did not. No scene was too vulgar for her; no gesture too outrageous. Whenever his oppression threatened to become too much for her, she could always fall back on this knowledge. Thus, she knew that so long as she maintained some outward show of propriety, then however much he might scold, however much he might rebuke, however much he might chide her, he wouldn't dare actually remove her from the ball for fear of her making a commotion.

Knowing the limits which were set upon her, then, Hermione had set out to enjoy herself to the outermost reach of those limits. That was not difficult. Of course, she had been to balls before, so they needn't try to pretend that she hadn't, but there was no denying that she had never been at anything as grand as *this!* And whatever her uncle said, she *knew* that she was the best dressed and quite the prettiest girl in the room (except, of course, for that Mrs. Welton. But she was a widow and *ever* so old, and she didn't dance, and she hadn't any money, and who cared about her *anyway?*). And the men all knew it, too. Wasn't her hand sought for every dance, and that by all the most presentable men? Didn't no fewer than four besotted youths lure her to the Conservatory for a heady mixture of kisses and protestations of devotion? Wasn't that handsome Lord Sandston answering to her every beck and call, and positively *begging* her to slip away from her uncle and Rachel some time to meet with him? Wasn't it a *glorious* ball?

Dawn was threatening to overcome the night when the members of the Ramsey and Arrington households all reached their beds. They had all had a grand time.

Six

By two o'clock the following day, the Arrington home was inundated with cards. The ball had, it seemed, opened a veritable floodgate through which poured earnest solicitations to balls, routs, picnics, and masquerades. The Season was so newly begun that their evening had served informally to declare it open, and numerous hostesses (particularly those with promising sons) had only waited to see whether Amelia Arrington was to be tolerated on account of her fortune or snubbed because of her color before sending out their own invitations. Lord Sandston's opening dance with his cousin having alerted the *ton* that the Arringtons were, at least for the present, showing a united face, he found himself similarly welcomed by many hostesses who had been previously inclined to ignore him as a penniless rattle. Thus began a round of amusements to which Stephen could squire his sister and cousin. Hezekiah did not approve of his nephew any more now than before, but he was so grateful to be thus relieved of the responsibility for attending social events which he considered both tedious and an affront to his religious convictions that he willingly turned over the role of chief escort to him, scarcely being seen in his family's presence from that time on.

Hermione Pendergast and Rachel Thomason, too, found themselves much in demand by many of the same hostesses and for much the same reason. Although Miss Pendergast's manners were deplorable, it was easy to view this as reflecting a charming *naïveté* in one who was not only (to be honest) *extremely* young but was also reputed to be nearly as wealthy as the Arrington girl and (to be more honest still) considerably more handsome. The patronesses of Almack's, indeed, gave serious thought to excluding *both* the heiresses from that club's hallowed precincts, but Lady Burrell had an ancient and unexpected *tendre* for Hezekiah Arrington and Sally Jersey for Peter Ramsey which procured vouchers for both and for Rachel and Persephone as well.

Inevitably, then, the inhabitants of the two households saw a great deal of each other in the days after Amelia's ball. The very next day, in fact, as Amelia and Persephone drove in the Park, Stephen riding by their side and gaily pointing out to his cousin such figures of interest as William Lamb, rising Whig politician, son of the notorious Lady Melbourne and husband to the even more notorious Caroline Lamb, they espied Miss Thomason, Miss Pendergast, and Mr. Ramsey riding in the distance. (Persephone felt a pang of envy; she herself would have preferred to be on horseback, but her cousin didn't ride.) The two parties converged near the Walk, and joined together. (Ramsey was torn between enjoying more conversation with the widow and discouraging Sandston's attentions to his niece, but decided that his presence might sufficiently repress his lordship that he would indulge his own fancy rather than gratify his instincts as a guardian.)

"Well met, ladies," Ramsey called out gaily. "I'd not

have thought to see you out after your dissipations of last night." Then, nodding, "Good day, Sandston."

Hermione smiled brilliantly at the entire Arrington party. She'd been sulking since they left the house over her uncle's decision to accompany Rachel and herself on this ride, convinced (rightly) that he did so primarily to keep an eye on her and resenting deeply this chaperonage. However, when it became clear not only that her uncle would permit them to ride alongside this open landolet but that his attention was sufficiently focused upon its occupants to distract him from herself, her volatile spirits soared. It would be untrue to say that she favored Lord Sandston over any one of a dozen gentlemen who'd expressed a flattering interest in her the previous night—her dances with him had reflected little more than a desire to irritate and flout Uncle Peter—but he certainly would make an admirable conquest. When he managed unobtrusively to maneuver his horse next to hers under the pretext of allowing her uncle to pay his respects to Miss Arrington, she giggled delightedly, and when he leaned over and said under his breath that she reminded him of a woodland sprite in her forest green habit with a pheasant feather perched cockily in her bonnet, she positively beamed.

Meanwhile, both Amelia and Persephone were delighted as well. Amelia had wished to advance her acquaintance with Mr. Ramsey in order to have an opportunity to speak with him further about her mother and Persephone, to whom she'd confided this wish, and was pleased to see it gratified. Both ladies, then, were warm in their greetings (a warmth on Persephone's part which Ramsey read as further encouragement to his scheme).

"Well met, indeed, Mr. Ramsey. And how did *you* survive your dissipations?"

"Miss Arrington, you should know that we men play the easy part at gatherings such as last night's—the burden falls all upon you ladies to amuse us, while a fellow such as myself may always excuse himself from dancing on the pretext of leaving it to the halflings." (Ramsey had not, in fact, danced, finding little time between his vigil over his niece and his pursuit of Mrs. Welton.)

Persephone interjected, "But I'm sure the effort to *appear* amused is sometimes quite as exhausting as the effort to be amusing, particularly," she added archly, "for a gentleman such as yourself who is beyond the pleasures of dancing."

"Ah, but it was no effort to be amused by Miss Arrington and Mrs. Welton, I assure you. Indeed, I awoke this morning at my accustomed time and spent several hours in the City before midday."

"You, then, are like my uncle, whom nothing tires and nothing keeps from his affairs?"

"Well, I can't lay claim to Mr. Arrington's virtues; he stands quite alone in my acquaintance in his capacity for work and attention to detail."

As Persephone had intended in turning the conversation to her uncle, this was precisely the opening which Amelia had been awaiting. "And was he always so thorough, Mr. Ramsey? You must know that every child has a great curiosity about her parents, and I've often wondered what my father was like as a young man, and if he were *quite* so devoted to business when my mother was still alive."

If Amelia was pleased at the turn the conversation had taken, Ramsey was disappointed, although too much of a gentleman to show it. He'd hoped to further his suit with The Welton; he found himself instead answering her cousin's questions about the late Mrs. Arrington. It was a discussion in which Persephone could play but little part and as it quickly became time for the two parties to go their separate ways, Ramsey had no more opportunity to converse with her that day.

More arose, however, almost immediately as Ramsey continued to accompany his niece, and Persephone her cousin, on a whirl of activities. Indeed, so assiduous was Ramsey in his attention to his ward that Society's interest was aroused. Miss Thomason was, after all, a reliable companion and Peter Ramsey was not known for spending his time in the round of amusements the Season provided. That he should accompany Miss Pendergast to private balls and to Almack's was expected, but that he should be seen at her side at the Venetian breakfast presented by Lady Holland or a balloon ascension in the Park was not. Slowly, the fact that he was often seen also in the presence of Miss Arrington and her beautiful cousin at these same affairs was noticed by more perceptive souls, and gave rise to considerable speculation. That he was in no hurry to marry had for some time been obvious—he'd four younger brothers and a tribe of nephews to carry on the family name, and had never been linked by rumor to any eligible virgin—but there was no saying that he might not finally have that, or some other, game in mind. But which was his object, the Heiress or the Beauty? *They* were rarely apart, so it made it difficult to guess. If the first, it seemed to most men a shabby thing. *He* didn't need her fortune. If the second, it seemed to most women almost equally shabby; there were marriageable girls enough and more who'd be all too ready to favor his suit without his looking to a widow, past her salad days and with no fortune to recommend *her.* And if his object were not marriage at all, then why was consummation of his plan so delayed? Still, Ramsey's motives, whatever they were, provided food for gossip and as gossip was the very stuff of which a successful Season was made, the *ton* were by and large grateful.

Ramsey's ward was similarly generous. No need to fear lack of scandal when *she* was about! Her court numbered in the dozens, and she was continually urging one or the other of them on to some kind of outrageous conduct. Poor Freddy Harris, indeed, was taken up by the Watch because he had, on her instigation, climbed in a second-floor window at the home of one of his rivals in a fruitless attempt to recover a corsage of hers that Hermione had given away. It was impossible to determine which gentleman she favored, but again the more percipient thought they discerned a preference for Lord Sandston despite (or, perhaps, because) of her guardian's patent disapproval.

Ramsey, no fool, knew himself and his ward to be observed, but cared little. He *was* bothered, though, by the fact that he was little farther along after two weeks of pursuit than he'd been after two days. He'd achieved an easy intercourse with both Amelia Arrington and her cousin and continued to believe the widow to be receptive to his advances, but she either was dull (which he did not credit) or coy; he simply could not manage to get her alone for long enough to offer her the *carte blanche* he intended. Indeed, he was becoming irritated by the situation and feared that he was beginning to appear ridiculous. There he was, dancing attendance on his ward and the widow as if he'd nothing better to do with his time while the widow, as it were, led him on with one hand and held him off with the other. He determined to make but one more push and, if The Welton continued to play the virtuous maiden, she'd find out her loss!

The very day upon which Ramsey reached this resolve, Rachel received a note from Persephone. "Rachel," it read, "tonight we are to enter the Holy of Holies; my uncle, through means best known to him, has procured us vouchers to Almack's, and means to accompany us. My brother, too, will be in our party. I know that you told me that Mr. Ramsey has received vouchers for you and Miss Pendergast as well; do you plan to attend this evening? Unless you've other plans, I entreat you to come. I was never there—my father was out of favor with Lady Jersey, I believe, and my husband with almost everyone—but I've been told that it is excruciatingly dull if one doesn't dance. I look forward to you presence, then, to rescue me from the tedium. (Amelia, who just entered the room, adds her pleas to mine.)"

In fact, Rachel and her cousin had no plans for that evening (which is to say that they had half a dozen invitations, none terribly alluring), and Hermione was eager to attend Almack's for the first time, an eagerness which the knowledge that Lord Sandston would be present fanned. Rachel doubted that that factor would work equally positively on Mr. Ramsey, however, and was surprised when he agreed with alacrity to escort the two ladies himself. This would, he thought, be The Welton's last chance.

The Arrington party arrived shortly before ten to find the rooms teeming. Persephone was looking particularly lovely in a muted lavender crepe gown with a high neck, relieved only by a simple but exquisite emerald pin which matched her green eyes and which her uncle had presented her that very day. The four wandered slowly together through the rooms, nodding here and there to acquaintances and coming at last upon Ramsey's party. They were still exchanging greetings when Amelia's hand was claimed by one of her admirers for the country dance then beginning and his lordship took advantage of the moment to claim Miss Pendergast's. Persephone, watching both couples forming part of a set, turned back to address a remark to Rachel, but found in the interim that both she and Uncle Hezekiah had wandered off, the one to procure a glass of lemonade and the other to greet Lady Burrell and to thank her for his daughter's and niece's admission. She found herself, then, alone with Mr. Ramsey, a matter which she viewed with only moderate satisfaction. She'd seen a great deal of the gentleman in the past few weeks, and her opinion of him was not enormously high. He was charming enough and frequently quite witty, but fatally addicted to high-flown compliment for which she had little taste. Indeed, as he seemed inclined to make her the object of his gallantry, and as she not only did not believe him to be serious but would not in any event have contemplated an alliance with any member of the late Captain Welton's set, she'd made something of a point of not being alone with him before. She held him in no particular aversion, however, and looked at him now with a friendly enough smile.

"I never see you dance, Sir. Don't you enjoy it?"

"Why would I wish to dance when you do not?"

There. That was just the sort of thing Ramsey always *was* saying. "Surely there are others more worthy of your attention than I?"

"Not one, I assure you."

What to say now? Really, the man was most irritating, and now he was staring at her in such a fixed manner that she hardly knew where to look.

"I know you believe my brother to be a sad fribble, but you must admit that he and your niece make a handsome couple."

"Hang your brother! Enough of this fencing, my dear. Lord knows neither of us is a child and both should know what we are about." And with that, and before Persephone could so much as say a word, Ramsey set out his offer to her in terms as explicit as they were generous.

All color drained out of Persephone's face as she listened. Had Ramsey been foxed, she might have understood how this offer came to be made, but the man was all too clearly sober. What *had* she done to make him think that this was anything but a deadly insult? Indeed, he seemed to think that she would find his conversation nothing out of the way!

Finally noticing her expression and her silence, Ramsey came at last to a halt, looking perplexed. Surely, he'd not misread the signals the woman had been sending him these past weeks? She was free to say no, of course, or even to bargain, but he'd hardly expected her to turn to stone at his mere proposal. Somewhat uncertainly, then, he said, "Well? Does my proposition interest you?"

Persephone took a deep breath, trying to master her voice. "I can only assume, Sir, that you are a lunatic whose secret has been kept by your family. I will spare my uncle the grief which this tale would cause him only on the condition that I never need see you again!" She was about to walk off, but turned back for an instant. "You are *despicable,* Sir!"

Ramsey was outraged. First the trollop had led him on and now she insulted him? If she did not wish to accept his protection, that was one thing, but this show of fury was quite another. He'd wasted two weeks (and some of his pride) on the widow, and to end it with nothing more than a scolding was intolerable. "Fine words, Madam, for someone with your history."

"My *history?* My history, sir, is an unexceptionable one. I was born a lady, married a gentleman, and I am now a widow."

Ramsey, having decided that if he could not gratify one passion, might as well enjoy another, was thoroughly enjoying the row by this time, and laughed. "You are certainly now a widow, and I have nothing to say to your birth. As to the rest, you must surely be aware that your late husband was in the habit of wagering you at cards and I take leave to doubt whether that qualifies him as a gentleman."

"*What!*"

"Oh yes. Whenever he had run out of more liquid

assets, Welton would lay a bet such as a dinner at your house, or an evening at cards. As you were notoriously among the most beautiful women in London, and as you were, at that time, rarely seen in Society, some of his more jug-bitten friends would take him up on the bets, and more than once, won."

As Persephone listened in mounting horror, Ramsey went on. "It was assumed that you were a party to these wagers, or at least knowledgeable about them, since Welton had moved in the best circles for years and no one could believe that he would bandy his wife's name about without at least her consent, if not her connivance. Indeed, it appeared to many to be a very neat way to raise the ready, and, frankly, as little was known about you personally but a great deal about your father, it was assumed that you were a willing participant in what was ultimately an innocent enough pursuit."

"You mean to tell me that there are *gentlemen* who would cover such a . . . such a *loathsome* bet!"

"Hardly loathsome, my dear. And remember, it *was* your husband who offered the bets."

Persephone, uncertain whether her predominant emotion was mortification or plain and simple rage, did not trust herself to speak. The conversation had taken place near the door to the ballroom, and at this last remark, she simply turned on her heel and stalked out of the room. Looking briefly about the hall to see that she was not observed, she walked from the hallway into a smaller withdrawing room where she picked up a particularly ugly vase and deliberately smashed it into the fireplace. She then carefully placed a bill from her reticule in the place of the vase, and returned to the ballroom and to Mr. Ramsey's side.

During her absence, Ramsey had wondered what would happen next. There was no denying that their fight had had much the same effect on him as a good thunderstorm on a close summer's day; he felt relieved, and somewhat exhilarated. The Welton was, if anything, even more beautiful than he'd thought, and he liked the fact that she clearly had her wits about her. He'd never favored stupid women; they bored him. And he by no means despaired of his conquest. For all of Persephone's outrage, he was still convinced that the baggage was no better than she should be. To Ramsey, it had been apparent from very shortly after he had met David Welton that the man was a thoroughgoing blackguard, if an amusing one, and he tolerated him simply because of his excellent judgment of horseflesh. What had been obvious to him should, he thought, have been equally obvious to Welton's wife, and he found it difficult to believe that Persephone was entirely innocent of her husband's true character. It was much more likely that her fury stemmed from being confronted unexpectedly with his knowledge of their little game and with her own frailty. A flaming temper went well with her red head, but it was more than possible that calm reflection would lead the lady to conclude that an alliance with a man who already knew her secrets was not without its advantages. When he saw Persephone reappear at the doorway, then, looking quite calm and clearly seeking him out, he was prepared to be greeted with a coy overture. Instead, Persephone favored him with an aloof small bow, and said, "Sir. I believe I must thank you for telling me this story; it's as well that I am aware of it. I further must forgive you your misapprehension as to my character which is, I fear, all too understandable given what you have told me of my husband. I would be grateful, however, if you would do me the honor to believe that this is the first I had heard of it, and if you would do me the further honor to treat me as a complete stranger from this point forward, as I shall treat you. Thank you." At that, she walked off and didn't speak with Mr. Ramsey again for the balance of the evening.

Seven

The next day dawned dull and gray and the inhabitants of Uncle Hezekiah's house felt as dull as the day itself. Even Amelia's normally serene spirits seemed oppressed, although she professed herself to have enjoyed Almack's a great deal more than she would have thought possible. After breakfast, when the cousins had retired to the charming morning room which looked out on the still-bare garden, she seemed so unusually thoughtful that Persephone made a concerted effort to overcome her own languor and discover what was the matter. Amelia, though, only laughed and insisted that Persephone was becoming as solicitous as her old governess. She was somewhat bothered, she said, by Stephen's pursuit of Miss Pendergast the previous night, asking in a slightly constrained tone whether she was correct in her thinking that it was not at all the thing for them to have danced four times together, but would not admit to any other ills. As the recent weeks had been spent in almost ceaseless commotion, Persephone decided that her cousin's preoccupation was simply a reaction to the successes and excesses of the preceding fortnight.

As to Persephone herself, she was honest enough to

acknowledge the causes of *her* discontent. Mr. Ramsey's insolence and his revelations had together deprived her entirely of her peace of mind, and Stephen's infatuation with Ramsey's niece, which appeared to be deepening, was simply the final straw. As to the one, there was little or nothing that she could do now to mend the wrong that her husband had done her other than to continue to show herself in society as a respectable female, a prospect she found singularly daunting. As to Stephen, there probably was little more that could be done about that. Were it not for the irritation which it was certain to cause Peter Ramsey, there was no question in her mind that she would have done her best to interfere with that particular flirtation. Stephen might talk as if he were a heartless fortune hunter, but she did not for a moment believe that he could truly be happy were he to marry just for a fortune even if that fortune came with a pretty face, and she could not for the life of her believe that a sane and sober Stephen could truly *love* Hermione Pendergast. (She tended, in fact, to think that the only proper mates for Miss Pendergast were to be found in one of His Majesty's more select prisons.) If she *were* inclined to intervene, a few words dropped in Rachel's ear would be most effective, but she could not imagine herself calling at Mr. Ramsey's house again. It seemed to her, then, that she was destined to live out at least the next months (if not, she thought gloomily, the next years) tormented by fears on the one hand that the *ton* might think too little of her, and on the other that Stephen might think too much of Hermione.

The young ladies had taken a belated breakfast, again not having reached their beds until near dawn, and were making desultory conversation while hoping that the sun would break through the clouds. The morning room was normally the most cheerful chamber of the house, decorated all in white and yellow with a delightful floral motif repeated in the chair coverings, curtains, and carpet, but this morning the dark sky imparted some of its own drabness even to the room. The sun had just scored its first small victory, winning a smile from the cousins, when they heard the unexpected but unmistakable sound of callers at the door. Each perked up a bit; their own company was dull enough in all conscience, and each unconsciously straightened her gown and her hair. They could not think who was likely to come calling this early; nearly everyone who ever *did* call on them had been at Almack's the night before and had probably not reached *their* beds until as late as they themselves. They were nonetheless more than generally surprised when Miss Thomason and Miss Pendergast were announced. They'd barely had time to exchange glances, though, when Hermione precipitated herself into the room, followed by Rachel at a more dignified pace.

"We just *had* to come, or at least *I* had to come and fusty old Rachel said I couldn't come alone because of it being improper though I can't for the life of me see what could be improper about calling on ladies or, in any event," Hermione paused for breath, "in *any* event, last night was just a lovely ball, don't you think, but we've all been doing nothing but dancing and I *do* miss the country and would you like to come to Richmond with us?"

Persephone, as prepared as she was to dislike anything to do with Hermione, and recognizing how little this sort of speech would endear the girl either to her guardian or to the sorts of older women whose favor it would do her well to curry, could not help but be amused at this ingenuous outburst. Indeed, she thought with some dismay, if this was the way Miss Pendergast habitually spoke to Stephen, she could see why he was taken with her. She doubted that he had the judgment to see that what was a charming assurance when the heiress was happy could turn within seconds into a shrewish explosion if she were crossed. Still, she smiled at the girl while Amelia, after offering them seats in one of the comfortable armchairs with which the room was dotted, responded, "I *am* pleased that Almack's met with your approval."

Hermione frowned at her. "Was that sarcasm? Uncle Peter says that I never understand when people are being serious and when they are making fun of me." She then went on, as if commenting on the weather, "Uncle Peter's a beast, and says that people are *frequently* making fun of me, but that I just don't know it and that I will *never* understand what they mean or be fit company for a rational gentleman if I don't start paying more attention to what *they* say and less to what *I* mean to say next, but none of the other gentlemen of my acquaintance seems to mind, and my governess always told me that the worst thing that a girl can be is tongue-tied, and certainly even Uncle Peter can't say that I am *that.*"

Here, Rachel interrupted. "Indeed, not your worst enemy could say that, my dear. But I believe you have said quite enough now." She then turned to Persephone and Amelia. "Really, I wouldn't have allowed my cousin to intrude on you this morning if I weren't convinced that we have all been rather too busy these past weeks, and could each enjoy a recruiting day in the country.

"As Mr. Ramsey's groom, who is remarkably knowledgeable about such things, promises us that after its gloomy start, today will be a particularly fine one, we determined to try out the new carriage which Mr. Ramsey so kindly presented to Hermione" (Rachel ignored Hermione's interpolation "Beast! He knew I wanted a phaeton. A *high perch* phaeton!") "and drive out to Richmond, and we wondered whether you two might perhaps care to join us."

Persephone was about to make her excuses when she realized that, in fact, a drive in the country might be just the thing to raise her spirits. Also, it struck her that it might well behoove her to gct to know Miss Pendergast a little better, if only to have a better idea of how best to combat her influence on Stephen, and that her opportunities for this might now be extremely limited. Turning to Amelia, she made a slightly comical face and said, "Cousin, I hope that you will not take it ill if I observe that you and I have been the most *uninspiring* company this morning, and I can't help but believe that we would both be the better for an infusion of new blood. What do you say to our accepting this kind offer, and let the tedium of our company be a warning to Miss Thomason and Miss Pendergast against such impulsive charity in the future?"

Amelia laughed. "Well, Miss Thomason, if my cousin hasn't put you off by her quite *devastating* honesty, for truly I believe that two such unexciting creatures could scarcely be found in all of London today, I will be most grateful. I've not seen Richmond yet and am told that the drive is most lovely, and the view quite the best to be found anywhere near town. I count on you to tell me all the most amusing anecdotes you know and thereby to camouflage my own stupidity."

Hermione had obviously been paying but scant attention to this exchange, and interrupted now to exclaim, "And I've the most *cunning* idea! Why don't we take up Mrs. Welton's brother to keep us company along the way! You know how Uncle Peter is forever prosing on at me for going about without proper escort, and I shouldn't like him to think that I have *jauntered* off to Richmond without a respectable gentleman to protect us." Her smile was a miracle of bland innocence, and Persephone wondered briefly whether the silly girl actually believed that any of her listeners thought that this idea had just come to her and was not the whole point of the venture from the start. In any event, now was as good a time as any to commence putting a spoke in *that* wheel.

"Miss Pendergast, dear, I sincerely doubt that your uncle would consider my brother a "respectable gentleman," as you put it, and in any event you surely can't believe that he is awake yet? Why, after leaving Almack's he probably went to three more balls and danced a dozen more times. I scarcely remember an evening during the past five Seasons when he hasn't attended a half-dozen affairs, and he is always so sought out that he spends the good part of every day resting his feet from their exertions of the previous night and preparing them for thc evening to come."

There was, in fact, some truth in this speech; Stephen was a fine dancer and spent many an evening flitting from ball to ball, always welcome (at least by those hostesses who did not hold themselves too high in the instep) because his good nature made him always willing to squire a spare damsel if necessary. However, Persephone's chief motivation had been to attempt to impress on Hermione the belief that her four dances the previous night with his lordship had been of no very great importance after all, and in that (perhaps unworthy) motive, she appeared entirely to have failed, as the heiress responded sunnily, "Oh, I'm sure that wasn't true *last* night. Stephen, Lord Sandston, I mean, told me *especially* that he couldn't bear to dance with anyone else after me, because I'm as light on my feet as a fairy, he said, and that was the only reason I favored him four times and *not,* as *some people* have said, because I'm one to tie my garter in public, but only because he said he wouldn't dance unless I *did* dance with him, and it would have been a shame to see him sit out all the evening, wouldn't it?"

"So you see, I'm quite sure that Ste . . . Lord Sandston didn't spend the whole night dancing, and would probably *love* to come to Richmond with us."

The sound of the knocker at the front door interrupted Persephone before she could respond, and the sound of Stephen's voice in the hall asking after his sister and his cousin caused her to frown in annoyance. Really, it was too bad of Stephen to have concocted this appointment, as he had so obviously done, and to use her and Amelia in this way! Rachel's expression showed that she had reached the same conclusion as had Persephone, but her grimace showed equally that she felt herself unequal to the task of stopping Hermione at this point in the proceedings. Before Persephone could reach any firm conclusion as to what she wished to do, Stephen had entered the room.

Far from appearing abashed at the three frowning (and one glowing) face which greeted him, the vision sent him into whoops. "If you don't look like three governesses and a runaway schoolgirl, I don't know what you *do* look like. Come now, ladies, surely it is not so very bad of me to wish to accompany not one, nor two, nor even three, but *four* Beauties on an expedition to the country on a fine spring day?"

"Stephen, it is *not* funny! Our uncle's house is no place for assignations, and well you know it."

"Perse, I know it so well that I suggest we leave immediately before Uncle gets wind of our presence and suggests we attend a prayer meeting for the good of our souls after our dissipations of last night." And then, when he was unable to coax a smile out of his sister, he turned to Amelia. "Come now, Cousin, I know that *you,* at least, are not going to make a Cheltanham tragedy out of what is, after all, no great thing. You wish to go to the country with me, don't you?"

Hermione chose this moment to speak. "I can't *think* what you are going on about, Lord Sandston. It's true that we were all about to leave for Richmond, though how you've guessed it I *don't* know, and we would certainly welcome your company, but all this talk of *assignations* is beyond *me.*"

"Now Miss Pendergast, one of the first rules of military strategy is to know when your plans have been discovered and to adapt yourself accordingly. I'm very much afraid that our clever scheme has been penetrated by these three very sage and very disapproving ladies, and unless we can convince them that our outing will do no harm, it will not take place."

At this, Persephone finally laughed. "I'm sure that no one here has any intention of making so much out of something so very little. If we ladies wish to go to the country for the day, I am certain that there is nothing to stop us, and nothing to stop you from accompanying us. I could only wish that you had not attempted to make such a mystery of it—it is the air of secrecy that is distasteful, as I'm sure Miss Thomason will explain to Miss Pendergast but not, I most sincerely hope, now. If we are to go, we had best go, and that's that!"

In fact Persephone, watching the mulish set of the heiress's mouth as the discussion progressed, decided that she had neither the taste nor the patience for dealing with another of the girl's scenes and that the impropriety, after all, had been in her making the appointment with Stephen and not in their actual plans. Rachel having reached much the same conclusion, only a few minutes more were needed before the company was on its way, the four women riding in the elegant open carriage and Stephen mounted on a fine roan hack, trotting merrily alongside. Rachel had packed a hamper for a picnic, and all five were quickly in high spirits.

The morning had indeed turned into a beautiful one, and Hermione, now that she had her way, proved a diverting companion although Persephone thought that it was a diversion that would soon pall. Her charm consisted largely of a mixture of *naïveté* and a certain selfish shrewdness that was not unamusing in a girl, however unattractive it was likely to be in a mature woman. The glances that she threw at Stephen, and he at her, did not encourage Persephone to believe that her brother perceived the heiress in quite the same way, however, and she couldn't help but wonder if he were really so devoted as he gave every appearance of being. If so, it was a sad tangle, and one of which she didn't readily see their way out.

Persephone was so preoccupied with her own thoughts that it was some time before she noticed a curious thing—although she could not say exactly how it came about, most of Miss Pendergast's most unattractive remarks were made in response to questions from Amelia. Indeed, once she set herself to paying some attention, it appeared to Persephone that Amelia was doing her best to draw out Hermione to display all her least appealing traits. Thus, she was at once amused and appalled when Amelia commented lightly about one of the more notorious blades with whom Hermione had spent some time at the Arrington ball to hear the girl respond with supreme ill-manners, "Oh, yes, I remember Mr. ffolliot. I would have supposed that anyone I met at your ball would be an acceptable partner, but his manner was so odd that I asked my uncle about him, and he told me that I was quite wrong."

Making matters worse, Hermione had appeared to recognize that this sounded rather rude, and had blundered on. "He told me that Mrs. Welton, as a widow, has *many* friends to whom I could not be introduced and even though that *did* sound just like more of Uncle Peter's fustian, I quite saw what he meant." Turning to Rachel, she added, "You see, you think I pay no attention at all to what you tell me, but I *do,* and I know that there are all *sorts* of things that a lady who is quite old can do that I can't."

Rachel, recognizing that Hermione's explanations would only become more embarrassing if she were allowed to continue, interrupted. "That is the closest I have ever hear you come to admitting that there is *anything* that you can't do, and I supposed that I must be grateful for that. However, you've said quite enough now."

Though perhaps the most egregious example, however, this exchange was not the only one of its sort, and by the time they reached the outskirts of the city, Persephone was convinced that Amelia had consciously set herself the task of encouraging the girl's worst excesses. Why she should be doing so, Persephone could not imagine, but she was pleased to see that Stephen appeared a bit shaken at some of his fancy's comments. Indeed, she thought, that could have been her cousin's motive, and how like Amelia it would be to go about thus subtly attempting to relieve Persephone's mind of a matter which she must know to be causing her considerable worry.

At just this point in her ruminations, Persephone suffered a most unwelcome surprise. Turning at the sound of hoofbeats coming up behind them in the road, she was shocked to see the unmistakable figure of Peter Ramsey approaching. A look of dismay crossed every face but that of Amelia, while Stephen whispered quickly to his sister before Ramsey was within earshot that she was on no account to allow the gentleman to challenge him to a duel as he was a notoriously good shot.

When he pulled up his horse, a raking chestnut, to the carriage, Ramsey could be seen to be suffering from extreme ill-humor. He had been out for a ride in the Park and had encountered one of his late sister's brothers-in-law, one of the several gentlemen to whom

Hermione had referred as an alternative guardian to himself. In her insinuations that there were several of her father's brothers who would be more than happy to take on the responsibility of so notable an heiress, Hermione was entirely correct, but as little as he relished the task of trying to govern Hermione, Ramsey did not wish to see his sister's only child turned over to any of her extremely vulgar paternal uncles. The fact that Hermione's inheritance came largely from her father's side of the family, the Ramseys having had no more than an excellent name and a genteel fortune before Peter Ramsey became involved in the Indian trade, made matters a trifle unpleasant. There was no question about the legitimacy of her father's will appointing him the girl's guardian and trustee. Still, there was equally little question that attacks might be made on the will were there to be any serious deficiencies in his guardianship of the girl. Relations between himself and her Pendergast uncles, then, were a bit strained, and hardly improved when this one, a city wine merchant of only moderate success named Sylvester, had hailed him loudly.

"Ramsey! What the devil do you mean by allowing my niece to make a figure of herself with young Sandston?"

Attempting to establish a civil tone, Ramsey pulled his horse up next to Mr. Pendergast's slug. The chestnut was, however, thoroughly unsuited for town riding and was held from bolting only by his rider's total concentration. Ramsey had taken him out solely to accustom him to London and had already concluded that it was a useless effort. He suffered, then, from a real apprehension that the brute might well kick out at the other's horse if he tried to keep him close enough for civilized conversation. He was therefore forced to rap out his answer both louder and more shortly than he would have chosen, "I haven't the slightest idea what you're talking about, Pendergast."

Nothing loath to bellow his reply, Sylvester responded, "That's just my point, old chap. You don't seem to know what's going on with the chit under your very nose. First thing this morning my wife tells me that her maid told her that Hezekiah Arrington's footman told the butler that that young blade has practically lived in Hermione's pocket since Hezekiah gave that party for his chit. Then, no sooner am I on my way this morning when I see, with my very own eyes" ("As if he could have seen it with anyone else's," Ramsey had remarked savagely to himself) "with my very own eyes my niece riding out with Sandston and no better escort than Rachel Thomason and Sandston's sister and cousin. And if you ask me" ("Which I didn't, nor would I!") "that sister is too pretty to be any better than she should be, and the cousin's too plain, setting aside the fact that she's nearly as dark as a heathen, and half of one if the stories I hear are true." He'd paused for a moment for breath, and then went on grudgingly, "As for Miss Thomason, I've nothing to say against her." Then he appeared to cheer up. "But I doubt she's got enough *nous* to combat what it's clear as the nose on my face is a conspiracy by Sandston's family to help him compromise our little Hermione."

Ramsey's immediate reaction was that the man was a fool; Hermione was obviously once again doing her best to make a public figure of herself, but that Miss Arrington or even Mrs. Welton would aid and abet her he sincerely doubted. Second thoughts, though, immediately assailed him. Certainly, the widow had looked angry enough when he saw her last to wish some revenge. She might well believe that this particular one would kill two birds with one stone, at once annoying him and, perhaps, ending in obtaining a handsome fortune for a brother to whom she was, by all accounts, devoted. As for Miss Arrington, he really knew nothing about her other than that she was Hezekiah's daughter, certainly a mark in her favor but not really of much use in letting him know how she would feel about a scheme that might appear to her simply in the light of helping her cousins to further their interests. As for Miss Thomason, he had complete faith in *her,* at least, but she might well be blinded by her partiality for her old friend.

Putting it all together, then, Ramsey was less inclined to damn Sylvester Pendergast as an interfering idiot and more inclined to consider his warning a timely one. Biting off the rejoinder that he had planned, then, he asked with a surprising degree of civility if Pendergast knew which way the company had been heading. Pendergast replied that he did; he had hailed his niece when he saw her, and she called out gaily that they were all on their way to Richmond, and wasn't it the grandest lark? Upon receipt of the further information that it had not been long ago that this encounter had taken place, Ramsey had paused only long enough to consider, and reject, the idea of returning to his stables for a more suitable mount, and had headed off after the young people, following the road upon which they were last seen.

He had ample time, but little leisure, to regret his decision, as the animal proved even harder to handle in the streets than he had in the Park. By the time he came upon the carriage, already some miles from Town, Ramsey's arms ached from holding the beast at check and his temper was in shreds. This condition was scarcely improved by the sight of Stephen Arrington bending solicitously over his niece as his own remarkably well-mannered horse trotted gently by her carriage.

Eight

Amelia was the first to find her voice, calling out gaily, "Why Mr. Ramsey, what a delightful surprise. From what my father has told me, I shouldn't have thought you one to join in such frivolities as a picnic, or I should certainly have insisted that we invite you—let me tell you that a party of four women and one lone man sadly feels the want of additional male companionship."

Seeing the thunderous expression on Ramsey's face, Rachel thought it wise to pick up Amelia's thread, and added, "Indeed, Sir, I had thought you planned only to ride early in the Park and then attend to business in the City—I wish I'd known you planned instead to take a long ride, for then we needn't have troubled Lord Sandston to attend us."

These noble efforts were, however, of no avail. Coming up to the carriage at a ragged canter, Ramsey looked hot, bothered, and extremely irritable, and was barely able to bring himself to exchange marginally civil greetings with the party before saying, in a voice which sounded peevish even to his own ears, "I do *not* enjoy picnics, and I *had* intended to spend today considerably more fruitfully than chasing about after my ward, but as she has chosen to behave in such a way as to subject me to impertinences from"—here, Ramsey paused, bethinking himself of the impropriety of casting aspersions at Hermione's paternal relations—"certain persons, I have been given no choice." Attempting with a notable lack of success to adopt a more dignified tone, he went on. "Miss Thomason, I will discuss this whole affair with you later. Now, however, I would request that you have the carriage turned around, and that we all return to London, where, it is to be hoped, I can salvage the remains of my day!"

Ramsey was aware that he was being tyrannical and even absurd, but he was also well aware that his difficulty in handling both his niece and his horse was making him look ridiculous, a situation which brought out the worst in him. Now that he was actually confronted with the picnic party, his original reservations about Sylvester Pendergast's warnings came back to him in full force—anything more innocent than this excursion could scarcely be imagined, and if he would not have chosen to have young Sandston playing cavalier, neither could he in all honesty find anything very sinister about it. Persephone Welton might not be the companion as he could wish for his ward, but Miss Thomason and Miss Arrington made up for any of her deficiencies if, indeed, any such existed which, after her parting shot to him the previous night, he had begun to doubt. Still, having come this far and laboring as he was under a strong, if ill-defined, sense of ill-usage, he was determined to have his way, and went on, "I should hardly have thought it necessary to point out that my niece, having flung her cap at Lord Sandston all last night, had best guard what remains of her reputation, or she might as well give up any idea of being received by any respectable Society!"

Persephone had originally planned to hold her tongue. She had little desire to exchange more words with Peter Ramsey, and felt in any event that her intervention was hardly likely to tell in either Miss Pendergast's or her brother's favor. She was also all too aware that Ramsey's strictures, if harsh, contained a grain of truth. Now, however, she could no longer restrain herself. "Such a piece of work over so very little! Really, Mr. Ramsey, if this is how you carry on your business dealings, I wonder that you are not at the mercy of every sharper in London, as credulous as you are! I don't know what has been said to you by what ill-natured person, but you can hardly object in all fairness to your ward spending a recruiting day in the country after the exertions of these past weeks!"

"I will thank you, Ma'am, to keep to yourself your opinions of what I can allow my ward—you are hardly the person from whom I would seek advice about polite behavior."

Stephen, recognizing his own equivocal position in all of this, had also resolved to play no role in the discussion, but that resolution had not taken into account the possibility that Ramsey would choose to insult his sister. "That will be quite enough, Ramsey. You will keep a civil tongue in your head when addressing a lady or I'll know the reason why; your unfortunate niece may have to put up with your Turkish treatment, but the same is not true of my sister."

Persephone had no desire to see the two men come to blows over her and attempted to intervene, saying soothingly, "Come now, I believe you are both getting carried away. Stephen, you shouldn't be so ready to see offense where I'm sure none was intended, and you, Mr. Ramsey . . ." Persephone was not really certain what else it was that she intended to say, and was never given the chance to finish her sentence. Just as she paused for breath (and for thought) Ramsey's horse decided that a rabbit which had just chosen to skitter across the road was the final provocation in a morning that had included all too many. Taking advantage of the slackening of Ramsey's strict attention to him, the animal suddenly reared and twisted himself around, clearly trying to unseat the rider whom he had long since decided he had no desire to carry.

Under normal circumstances, this sort of display in his mount would have done little more than briefly distract Ramsey. An excellent horseman, Ramsey had ridden many a bad-tempered brute without mishap. However, circumstances now conspired against him. The long period of constant attention the horse had required had taken some toll, and there was no denying that Ramsey was tired. (His return from Almack's long after three o'clock in the morning played its part as well.) Further, his attention was thoroughly taken up by the argument in which he'd been engaged and, to top it all off, the horse had managed to maneuver itself between the carriage and Stephen's horse, giving Ramsey little room to let him thrash about into exhaustion. Still, for a moment it appeared that Ramsey's iron hand on the bridle would bring the animal under control, when suddenly the beast crashed into the carriage, pinning Ramsey's leg. Stephen's mount reared as soon as the other did, leaving him helpless to assist until he could quiet his horse, but he saw immediately that something was seriously wrong. Ramsey's grip with both his knees and hands had obviously weakened, and the horse was wrenching about all the more violently.

The women in the carriage could see more clearly than could Stephen, whose view was blocked by the body of the horse, what was wrong. Ramsey's leg was hanging down at an odd angle, obviously broken, and Ramsey himself had turned quite white. Hermione began to scream, while both Rachel and Amelia turned pale, and looked about them helplessly. John, the coachman, his own horses pawing the ground and tossing their heads restively, called out to Stephen.

"I'm that sorry, your lordship, but I daren't let go of the team or they'll as like as not take off at a run."

"That's right, man," Stephen shouted back. "On no account leave the horses. Lord! The last thing we need is another accident."

Everyone but Stephen, still trying to hold his bucking mount, and Ramsey, now swaying dangerously on his, appeared frozen in place, when suddenly Persephone leapt down from the carriage and, before her brother could guess what it was she intended, grabbed for the horse's bridle. She was immediately knocked down, luckily falling some feet away from the thrashing hoofs, but was up again so fast that Stephen had time now only to shout at her not to be mad. Her second attempt was rewarded with more success than her first, and she was able actually to catch hold of the animal's bit and forcibly prevent him from rearing yet again. During that brief moment when Persephone had him under her control, Stephen, his own horse finally responding to his command, was able to reach in and take the bridle from the other side. Held now on both sides, the wretched beast had not yet played his last trick, though. Balked from rearing, the animal lashed out with his leg and caught Persephone full on hers. She shrieked in pain, and fell. At almost the same moment, Ramsey finally fainted dead away, and slipped to the ground beside Persephone.

Silence now reigned. Even Hermione had stopped her hysterical screaming, staring down with her companions, wide-eyed, at the sight of the two casualties. A trickle of blood ran down Persephone's cheek from a scratch near her eye which she must have gotten when first knocked down, and that was the only color in either face. Ramsey's horse, satisfied with the havoc he had wrought, wandered quietly to the side of the road and began tearing at the grass with relish.

Amelia spoke in a strained voice. "Cousin Stephen,

you are closer than we are—can you see whether they are breathing?"

At that, Stephen started as if suddenly awakening. "Yes, of course they're breathing, but they both look to be in a bad way. Can one of you get down from the carriage to hold my horse?"

Amelia slipped down, and Stephen dismounted, handing his horse's reins to her. He knelt first by his sister, feeling quickly for a pulse. He nodded to Amelia, and smiled in what he hoped was a reassuring way, and then moved on to Ramsey. The latter, though, had already begun to stir, and before Stephen reached his side, his eyes flew open. He looked about him in a dazed way for a moment, and then pronounced quite clearly, "Hell and damnation," before fainting once again. Stephen could not help but smile at this, and announced with some relief that at least one of the victims appeared to be reacting much as could be expected. Persephone, too, began to stir at that moment, and opened her eyes with a gentle moan.

Her brother was beside her immediately. "Perse, it's me, Stephen. Do you know where you are?"

"No. Yes. I don't know." This, softly, and then, louder, "Stephen? Oh, it hurts so, Stephen. Make it stop hurting."

"Yes, darling, certainly." He took her hand, and then looked about helplessly. Wordlessly, Amelia motioned for Rachel to get down from the carriage and take his lordship's horse, and when she had done so, went to kneel by Persephone's side. Taking her cousin's other hand, she said softly, "Perse, this is Amelia. Your cousin Amelia. Can you tell us if you can move your leg at all?"

"Move my leg? No, of course not." Persephone, peevish in her pain and confusion, seemed to find this a ridiculous question. "It's broken. Can't you tell?"

Adjuring her cousin to turn his head, Amelia unceremoniously lifted Persephone's dress to view the injured limb and understood at once why Persephone had thought the question a silly one. The leg was quite obviously broken, bent at an angle no human leg was meant to bend. As the same was true of Ramsey's leg, there was no question that their most pressing need was to get the sufferers out of the sun and to some place where they could rest and be made more comfortable while they awaited medical attention.

Amelia and Stephen consulted quickly together. There was bound to be an inn somewhere nearby, and a quick question to John confirmed that he knew of a very respectable, if not very elegant, house no more than a mile or two away, down a small road that branched off from the main one. That house, too, would probably be the best source of information as to where to locate a doctor. Rachel suggested that if they all worked together, they could lift both their patients into the open carriage, and allow each to lie upon a seat. Stephen could ride ahead to warn the landlord of their descent and to begin the search for a doctor, while Ramsey's horse, the source of all their woes but nonetheless not to be abandoned, could be tied to the back of the carriage. The three women could then, she said, walk alongside the carriage which could not, in any event, proceed at any faster than a walking pace, since that would jolt the passengers too much.

At this point Hermione's evil genius urged her to raise an objection. "Walk? For nearly two miles? You must surely be joking, Rachel. Setting aside the heat and the dust, I'm wearing sandals that were hardly meant for exercise! No. I'll tell you what. John Coachman must drive us all as quickly as he can to this inn, and then come back for Uncle Peter and Mrs. Welton." Seeing the looks on her companion's faces, Hermione blushed, and said, "Oh, no, of course, someone must stay with the two of them. Miss Arrington can do that, can't she"—and, her voice rising dangerously—"she's *used* to all this dreadful heat, and I am not!" And with that, the Beauty burst into tears.

Before anyone else could say anything, Rachel responded. "Hermione, dear, you are being absurd, as you very well know. I know all of this has upset you greatly, but do try for a little conduct. You must understand that in this case the needs of Mrs. Welton and your uncle come first. Indeed, I know you do, and simply spoke without thinking."

At this, Hermione looked up with rather a stubborn expression, but a quick glance at Stephen made her bite back her intended reply, which was simply that she didn't care very much *what* happened to her uncle, and while she was very sorry for Mrs. Welton, she did not know her so well that she would choose to sacrifice her own comfort (and, she might add, her carriage) to her. However, while not a very clever girl, Hermione was not completely insensitive to the impression she made on others, particularly when those others were handsome young men, and there was no doubt that the impression she was making on Lord Sandston was far from a favorable one. So, instead of lashing out, Hermione hung her head in a singularly taking gesture and replied in a small voice that of course her cousin was right and that she had simply spoken from irritation of nerves. She graciously begged everyone's pardon and jumped quickly and gracefully down from the carriage, asking in what way she could be of help.

Stephen, shaken by Hermione's brief display of temper, was so preoccupied with his sister's predicament and relieved that at least one problem had been solved that he took the apology largely at face value and smiled gratefully at her. Rachel and Amelia exchanged glances, but began immediately to arrange the cushions in the carriage so that they would be most comfortable for the two invalids. Once that task was accomplished,

Stephen lifted Persephone into the carriage without any difficulty. Ramsey, predictably, posed more of a problem, but when John Coachman spoke up to suggest that if Miss (meaning, in this case, Hermione, who was a very pretty whip), would come up to hold the horses, he had no doubt that he and his lordship could manage the gentleman together, matters arranged themselves satisfactorily. Pausing only to get more specific directions to the inn, Stephen then took off down the road at little less than a dead run, leaving the coachman and the ladies to make their own arrangements. These were soon complete (including the tying of the now peaceful horse to the back of the carriage), and the cavalcade began slowly to move forward.

Nine

It was nearly an hour later when the carriage, accompanied by three hot, dusty, and testy young women, pulled into the small yard of The Green Man. The inn was, in fact, nearer two miles than one from the scene of the accident, and it had long since been borne in on Amelia and Rachel that Hermione's comments about her footwear, however petty and inappropriate they may have seemed, had the virtue at least of strict accuracy. None of the women had left home that morning planning on a long walk, and each was bitterly regretting the fashion that called for a lady of breeding to tread on gossamerlike sandals. Each was badly blistered; Amelia's feet were actually bleeding.

In all fairness, their regrets were hardly limited to the mundane question of feet. Even Rachel and Amelia found themselves in less charity with each other than they would have believed possible, the effects of a long and wearisome trudge having brought out whatever there was of the naggy in both of their tempers. They were united, however, in wishing Hermione at Jericho, or Timbuktu, or, indeed, anywhere, so long as it was sufficiently far away. No sooner had Lord Sandston ridden away, hell for leather, than Hermione had turned to Rachel and said, in a thrilling voice, "Once this *escapade* is complete, I shall *demand* that Uncle Peter rid me of the companionship of one who obviously does *not* have my best interests at heart, and find me a companion who is capable of entering into my concerns." Ignoring Rachel's glare, she went on. "Despite what *some people* so clearly choose to think, it was *not* that I am selfish or uncaring, but only that I wished, *unlike certain people* to be practical and not to show off my graces to *certain people* of whose attentions *those people* are obviously *jealous.*"

When Rachel was so unwise as to attempt to answer this farrago of nonsense, Amelia had interrupted sharply. "That is all well and good, but you two had best delay your bickering so that we may be on our way before my cousin and Mr. Ramsey suffer some further harm from lying out in the carriage in the full glare of the sun." Rachel, biting back a retort, was given full time to consider the fact that it does not in the least ameliorate the sting of a reproof to realize that the reproof is entirely just.

Hermione's suggestion that perhaps she should drive the carriage while the coachman walked was greeted with dead silence, and as even she knew quite well that she could not be counted on to keep the team at the steady slow walk that was called for, she simply bit her lip, and started off with the others. A moan from Persephone elicited the suggestion from Hermione that she should ride in the carriage to succor the sufferers, but she subsided once again when Rachel pointed out that she would have to sit or kneel on the floor of the carriage in order to keep her balance, and that that would doubtless ruin her dress, a new and favorite creation that she had worn to impress Lord Sandston. After a few minutes of silence, Amelia spoke up again. "Perhaps it *would* make sense for us to take turns riding on the floor of the carriage."

"You are free to do whatever you like," Rachel had snapped at her, "but for myself, I don't see that we can do either your cousin or Mr. Ramsey any good, as we have with us neither anything to shade them nor any water." Warming to her task, and grateful for a chance to return Amelia's reproof, she'd added, "In any event, we would be more likely than not to fall against one of them at some unevenness in the road and cause them additional pain."

Amelia, by then already limping noticeably, acknowledged the probable truth of that, but replied in a voice perilously close to a whine, "There is no reason to bite *my* nose off," and a resentful silence once again reigned.

From that point on, that silence was broken largely by the accelerating complaints of Hermione, complaints which, as the hour dragged on, were increasingly accompanied by lachrymose observations on the lack of interest shown by anyone for *her* well-being, including those to whom it should have been a primary concern. Indeed, by the time the inn was reached, anyone listening to Hermione would have been excused for thinking that Uncle Peter and Mrs. Welton had conspired together to cause the accident, out of nothing but a small-minded desire to ruin her proposed day of pleasure.

Throughout the hour, Persephone and Ramsey had both continued to appear largely unconscious, although an occasional sound from one or the other assured the listeners that both were still alive, at least. Indeed, Ramsey had, at one point, stirred and tried to sit up, asking querulously where he was and what the devil was going on, but he had seemed reassured by Rachel's reply that he was going to the doctor to have his leg seen to, and had laid his head down again. The coachman, in a better position to see his injured passengers, reassured the walkers that both were lying still and not worrying at their legs, and as Rachel's comment that there was, in fact, nothing that they could do to increase Persephone and Ramsey's comfort was obviously true, Amelia and Rachel were able to concentrate most of their attention on their own woes. (Hermione would have done so in any case.)

By the time they reached the sign of The Green Man, all the footsore travelers desired nothing so much as a quiet seat in the shade, a cool glass of lemonade, and a footbath. No such balms awaited them, however. As they turned into the innyard, they were greeted by the sight of the landlady standing in the doorway and shrieking to her unseen husband, "Lord a' mercy, Tewks, if they aren't here already and the young gentleman not back with the doctor." Continuing in a raucous squawk, she went on, "Well *I'll* not doctor them, and you can take my affidavit on that." (They were later to find that Mrs. Tewks, having once been a witness in a law case, frequently employed this expression as her means of reminding others of her distinction.) Rachel and Amelia, hearing this, stared bleakly at each other, but surprisingly, it was Hermione who took the matter in hand. She strode forcefully up to the landlady, a tall, gawky sort of woman—Hermione herself was variously described, depending on the source, as sadly lacking in inches or as being as small and delicate as a fairy—and planted herself in front of her.

"My good woman. No one is asking you to doctor anyone, but if you don't get out of that doorway and allow us to come inside out of this dreadful heat, I shall personally *slay* you *with my own hands.*" And then, as Mrs. Tewks stared down at her in some understandable astonishment, Hermione shook her fist at the woman, and went on, "Mrs. Welton is bleeding all over my carriage." That was an exaggeration, although it was true that Hermione had noticed that a spot of blood from Persephone's cut cheek had stained the brand-new cushions of her brand-new carriage. "My uncle is dreadfully pale, which is *most* unlike him and while I do *not* like him, whatever some people may say about my duty, I do *not* want him to die in my carriage; my feet hurt and I've been scolded and *scorned,* and *I WANT TO SIT DOWN!*"

At that, Mrs. Tewks meekly moved aside. As Rachel and Amelia privately considered that Hermione was fully capable of coming to blows with the woman had she frustrated her further, they could only applaud the landlady's good sense, and hope to take advantage of the breach in her defenses that this latter-day Joan of Arc had wrought. Before Mrs. Tewks could recover, then, Rachel had said in a voice that resounded with decisiveness, "You will excuse my cousin, I'm sure, when you understand how overwrought we all are from these dreadful events. For now, however, we require two rooms, both preferably well shaded; cooling drinks both for ourselves and, more importantly, for Mrs. Welton, whose brother, Lord Sandston, you have already met, and for Mr. Ramsey, both of whom are badly injured; a private parlor for Mr. Ramsey's ward"—nodding in the direction of Hermione—"and some assistance in getting Mrs. Welton and Mr. Ramsey to their rooms. I'm certain Lord Sandston warned you that these would be our requirements and that you have arrangements well in hand, so if you will just tell us what to do and where to take our friends, I will be most grateful."

Lord Sandston had, in point of fact, made a singular mull of things. He had descended on the inn like a whirlwind, pulling into the small, sleepy yard in a cloud of dust, calling out that he would be followed by a party with two injured people, and asking where the nearest doctor could be found. Considering it both unnecessary and vulgar to puff his own consequence, he had not bothered to identify himself but had only mentioned that the injured parties were his sister and a Mr. Ramsey. As he had gone on in his hurry to say that a room would be needed for them, Mrs. Tewks had received the understandable but erroneous impression that the sister was Mrs. Ramsey. She had, however, no particular desire to put herself about for the sake of an unknown Mr. and Mrs. Ramsey of who-knew-where, capable of paying no one-knew-what. That the gentleman on the horse was something of a swell was obvious, but his marked failure to drop any blunt to ease the path of those who were following him did not lead Mrs. Tewks to believe that he was, as she put it in her own mind, the right *kind* of swell. In her own way, Mrs. Tewks was remarkably democratic in her outlook, having little use for what she called sniffy-snaffy sorts of gentry. Her only concern was with who would pay her, and her experience was that her best trade came from young Pinks who were not, perhaps, of the highest *ton,* but were anxious to show themselves off to the world as if they were. The exquisite cut of Stephen's coat, then, which Mrs. Tewks was quite capable of appreciating, and the fine lines of his horse, which she also took in at a glance, meant considerably less to her than a lavish tip would have done. It would not be fair to say that she ignored the shouted commands entirely, but she had certainly not bestirred herself to any great extent.

(Although it never would have occurred to Stephen to have made a point of introducing himself as *Lord* Sandston or to have entered into a discussion with the woman of the size of Peter Ramsey's enormous fortune, he was aware that he should have given the landlady some monetary advance for her trouble. The problem was that he had left the house that morning with very little cash on him; he was, as usual, in dire straits and only carried with him so much of the ready as it seemed likely that he would need. In point of fact, he had little more than a few guineas. As he was very much afraid that he would have to pay the doctor out of that small sum before any money could be brought back from Town, he did not wish to squander the little cash he had at the inn. It was apparent that there would be time enough and more for money to be brought.)

To all appearances still dumbfounded by Hermione's unexpected attack, Mrs. Tewks had received Rachel's orders with all the animation of expression of a Guernsey cow. Actually, however, she was busy all the while taking in not only the cut of my ladies' gowns (including the elaborate one worn by the little termagant) but also the appearance of the carriage, the overbred bit of blood and bone tied to the back of it, and the elegant appearance of the invalids, neither of whose injuries and dust could disguise their obvious membership in that group which was broadly classified as Quality. These observations, combined with her opinion that only a great deal of money could have protected the vixen who had accosted her from the wrath of all she met, led Mrs. Tewks to decide that there was good money to be made from this unlikely party and, seeming to come alive, she curtsied to Rachel before turning back into the house to shout, "Tewks. Stop lazing about and come lend a hand with the gentleman as was hurt."

Amelia, believing that it was Rachel's cool head and authoritative manner which had brought about this sudden acquiescence, smiled an approval at Rachel which the latter, fully believing herself to be deserving, took in very good part. Mrs. Tewks, then, was all unwittingly the source of a reconciliation between those two ladies which might otherwise have taken some time to achieve, a good deed for which, it is to be feared, she would never receive the proper credit.

Having made his appearance, Tewks was found to be a very large and powerful gentleman who took one look at Ramsey and grunted. "I can lift that 'un without any help, thank you." Turning to the carriage, he added, "You, Coachman. You look to the lady."

An ostler having appeared to take care of the horses, John Coachman did just that, although not without some misgivings as to whether Mr. Tewks could really carry Peter Ramsey's fourteen stone alone. He might have spared himself the worry—Tewks, a former blacksmith who had married above himself, had no more trouble with Ramsey than the other did with Persephone. The two men, then, followed Mrs. Tewks up a broad staircase carrying their respective burdens, and deposited them in the rooms the lady indicated. If neither was, as requested, shaded, at least both appeared to the critical eyes of Rachel and Amelia to be clean and well cared for, and neither faced directly on the yard and so, it was to be hoped, would be reasonably quiet.

A brief consultation led Amelia to remain with Persephone while Tewks and Rachel did what they could to make Ramsey comfortable. As that included cutting the boot off his now badly swollen leg, it is to be doubted whether Ramsey himself would have characterized their activities in that way. Tewks showed himself surprisingly handy, however. Seemingly taking a liking to Rachel, he grew almost loquacious. "You see, Miss, this ain't so very different from shoeing an unwilling horse. I was used to be a blacksmith, you see, and I'd plenty of experience with holding things steady as what didn't *want* to be steady, if you get my meaning."

Ramsey, who passed in and out of consciousness during the proceedings, awoke once again when it was over, and professed himself grateful. He drank some of the lemonade that had been prepared (of which Rachel had already drunk thirstily), and said, "Now, if you please, give me a round tale as to exactly what had happened to lead me to this predicament. To be frank,

I remember little from the moment that blasted beast threw himself against the carriage."

When he heard of Mrs. Welton's intervention in his behalf and her own injury, his already pale countenance turned a shade more white, but he said nothing, only closing his eyes once again. Rachel was surprised; she would have expected some expression of gratitude, but was too weary and footsore herself to give the matter much thought. Having done what little could be done for her patient, she sat back in her chair, closed her own eyes, and thought longingly of a bath and bed.

In Mrs. Tewks's second-best room (Mrs. Tewks believing firmly that the *best* room should be reserved for gentlemen who were likely to be paying the shot) Amelia had, similarly, settled Persephone into her bed, held her head up so that she could drink some lemonade, and subsided gratefully into the chair that had been provided her. She even went so far as to take off her sandals, feeling that neither Tewks nor the doctor nor her cousin Stephen were likely to be scandalized by her bare feet, and that another minute in those instruments of torture would reduce her to screaming hysterics. Indeed, that very thought had just crossed her mind when she was unpleasantly brought to those same aching feet by the sound of a voice rising with a dangerous hysteria. It was, of course, Hermione.

"I suppose I am to sit alone in this *loathsome* little parlor until I am *dead* with thirst, *not* to speak of hunger since this *was* to be a picnic party and I did *not* eat a large breakfast."

Closing her eyes briefly, Amelia steeled herself to go downstairs and deal with the girl, when she heard the voice of Tewks saying soothingly, "Now, Miss, it's a right shame that you haven't been taken care of yet, and I'll speak to my good wife about it right away, don't you worry about *that.* Would you be wanting some lemonade and some cold meats?"

Mollified by the landlord's tone, Hermione sniffed, and responded that some fruit would also be acceptable. She then lapsed into silence for which Amelia (and Rachel, similarly listening for the sounds of an explosion in Ramsey's room) could only be profoundly grateful. Both women silently blessed Mr. Tewks for a tact which neither would have guessed that he possessed. In fact, Tewks was not tactful, but simply enormously taken with the tiny Fury who had so fearlessly assailed his wife, a woman of whom Tewks himself stood in considerable awe. Explaining the matter later to his particular crony, Mr. Featherstone of the rival White Horse, Tewks had put the matter this way.

"So there she was, this little thing that couldn't have stood no higher than five feet tall, and there was the missis, looming over her like Gog and Magog all rolled up in one, and what does she do but *shake her fist* right in the missis' face! If I had died at that moment, I'd have died a happy man." Mr. Featherstone allowed as how it must have been a rare treat, passing the story on to *his* particular crony, the barber Mr. Whitehead, who passed it on to each of his most select customers, until the legend of Little Miss had grown to such proportions that, had Hermione but known it, there was scarcely a home or business establishment for miles around in which she would not have been welcomed as a heroine.

Hermione, of course, did *not* know it. This was, as all of her relations would have been quick to point out, just as well, as her head was quite swollen enough by what she had decided was the rare presence of mind that had so signally distinguished her from Rachel and Amelia when confronted by That Woman. Indeed, so convinced had she become that it was only her willingness to brave the Ogress that had led to the party being taken into the inn at all, that by the time Stephen arrived with the doctor some half-hour later, a refreshed and rested Hermione was able to tell him, in what she believed was all honesty, that she had arranged everything so that the sufferers should have the best of care and attention.

He smiled at her, commenting in a fond voice that would have induced unbridled fury in his sister had she heard it, that this was just what he would have expected of her, and turned to lead the doctor upstairs. He was somewhat taken aback when Hermione became petulant. "You are not going to leave me alone *again?* Surely Rachel and Miss Arrington are upstairs and can talk to the doctor. They don't need *you.*"

Still largely distracted by his concern for his sister, Stephen paid little attention, but simply promised that he would not be long. He then turned to lead the doctor upstairs.

Persephone and Ramsey were exceptionally lucky in the doctor who attended them. Dr. Traherne was an older man, recently retired from an active practice in London, who had decided that a slower pace would suit his disposition better. He was extremely skillful, indeed much more so than Stephen had feared he would be able to find out of the city, and he examined his two patients quickly, gently, and with an obvious competence that allayed Stephen's worst fears. He went in first to see Persephone, who was lying awake, pain creasing her forehead. After a brief examination, Dr. Traherne smiled reassuringly and announced that the break appeared to be a fairly simple one. Warned by his lordship of the nature of the injuries he was to treat, he had brought with him all that he needed to set the bone, but warned the patient that it was likely to be quite painful. He ventured to suggest, therefore, that however little the lady might like it, she would be best off consuming a large amount of alcohol before he went to work on her, smothering Persephone's protests with the comment that neither her brother nor her cousin was likely to reveal anything that she might say while in her cups. When Amelia joined her voice to the doctor's and Stephen's in urging this course of action, Persephone yielded, and the doctor had left her wrinkling her nose over a beaker filled to the brim with Mrs. Tewks's best rum.

Dr. Traherne's report on Mr. Ramsey was less comfortable. Due, no doubt, to the angle at which the leg had been pinned, his break appeared more complex and the doctor felt obliged to warn him that he was in for a lengthy convalescence, and might be left at the end of it with some limp, although nothing, he added, which should interfere with his riding or sporting pursuits. He gave Ramsey the same advice he had given to Persephone, and found it was taken with considerably better grace. Leaving the one patient to his rum, then, Dr. Traherne had returned to the other, to find her gazing owlishly over the rim of an empty glass, ready, she said, for anything the doctor could do to her. In the event, neither her inebriated state nor the doctor's skillful work could save Persephone from experiencing considerable pain as her leg was set, and Stephen, who seemed to feel it almost as much as his sister did, could only be relieved when she passed out just before the job was done. The doctor, finishing his work quickly and neatly, agreed that it was perhaps just as well, and commented cheerfully that Persephone was now likely to sleep for at least several hours, just the thing she needed. Performing his work equally handily on Ramsey, Dr. Traherne saw his second patient of the day faint, and left him, similarly, to sleep.

With both Persephone and Ramsey seemingly safely unconscious, Dr. Traherne had suggested that they all retire to the parlor to discuss what else needed to be done. He presumed that the young lady whom he'd observed on his arrival was also of their party, and she would no doubt be relieved to hear that there appeared to be little permanent harm to be feared from the accident. While at least two of his listeners doubted whether Hermione cared a fiddle about the victims' well-being, Stephen responded quickly and with an air of concern that they were beasts to have left the child in ignorance for so long, and rushed headlong down the stairs. If Hermione, when seen, did not present the appearance of one worn down by worry—she was nibbling at a bowl of sweetmeats which Tewks had somehow procured for her and regaling him with the story of a riding accident which *she* had suffered only two years earlier in which she was saved from considerably more serious injuries than Mrs. Welton had sustained only by her cool head and consummate horsemanship—she at least had the sense to listen with what appeared to be rapt attention to Stephen's description of both his sister's and her uncle's conditions, and to express herself very prettily on the subject of her hopes for their speedy recovery.

It is true that her temper nearly got the better of her once again when it was decided that she and Rachel would ride home in the carriage to make arrangements for Ramsey's valet and Persephone's and Amelia's abigails to return to the inn with such luggage as their respective master and mistresses were likely to need for several weeks' stay at The Green Man, the doctor strongly urging against any plan to move either of the patients any sooner than that. Wouldn't it make more sense, she asked, for Lord Sandston to accompany her back to town so as to be able to break the dreadful news directly to his Uncle Hezekiah? When told by his lordship that that was very thoughtful of her, but that he couldn't think of leaving poor Ramsey without a man to look after him, she'd been about to reply that she didn't see why *Ramsey's* wishes should be given any higher priority than her own, since it had been his implacable desire to Tyrannize over *her* which had led to the entire predicament. She recognized from Stephen's tone, though, that he was quite decided, and she changed her mind. Instead of the projected speech, then, she simply smiled cheerily, promising that she and Rachel should be as quick about their tasks as was humanly possible. Rachel, forbearing to point out that it was unlikely that Hermione would bestir herself in the least to help make the myriad of arrangements that would be necessary, took a weary but fond leave of Amelia and Stephen and, John Coachman having been kindly but firmly detached from a pint of Tewks's best bitter, the carriage was seen off. It was unlikely that they would reach Town much before nightfall, and less likely still that either the servants or the baggage would arrive before the next day, so Stephen and Amelia resigned themselves to the wearisome task of sitting up all night with their patients, with not so much as the prospect of a change of clothes come morning to cheer them.

Ten

Some hours after Hermione and Rachel had left the inn, Amelia stood by the window in Persephone's room watching a glorious sunset. She was thinking, in no particular order, of how lovely the orange-tinted sky looked; how delicate the scent of the early spring flowers was; how very hungry she was; and how her feet ached. Her patient was still. Indeed, Persephone had scarcely stirred during the whole of the afternoon, and while Amelia knew that her poor cousin was going to awaken with a most unaccustomed hangover, she could only be glad that the good doctor's prescription appeared to be working so well as there was nothing that Persephone needed so much as sleep. Her gaze wandering over to the bed, Amelia tried to trace Stephen's features in his sister's much more delicate ones, but other than some similarity about their finely shaped mouths, there was little to tell that the two were siblings. Perhaps, Amelia thought, it was because one so rarely saw Stephen's face in the sort of repose that was one of Persephone's most pronounced characteristics. Indeed, she thought with a slight smile, while Persephone looked like nothing so much as a Raphael Madonna (or, perhaps, one by Titian, in deference to her hair, although

Amelia could not for the moment think of whether Titian had *done* any Madonnas), Stephen reminded her of nothing so much as a peasant or *tavernier* as painted by Velázquez, to whose works she had only recently been introduced. His dark eyes and hair, indeed, gave him a Spanish look, while the restless energy that seemed to keep him from ever being completely still defined him as truly as Persephone's restfulness did her.

As if echoing her very thoughts, Stephen's voice suddenly was heard from the doorway, whispering in deference to Persephone, but nonetheless brimful with impatience. "Confound it, Cousin, this playing at sick nurse is nothing but a sham, and so I shall tell the next female who tries to impose on me with stories of the great virtue of the female sex in being the ones usually to undertake this arduous task. I don't know about Perse, but Ramsey hasn't so much as stirred a finger in over an hour, and if you ask me, he ain't likely to for another ten. Lord! My hat is off to the man. I believe he drank as much rum as I could have in a day, and thanked the doctor handsomely for his work in the bargain. That was before he passed out, of course; still, it was an impressive performance. I'd be proud to think that Persephone matched it but none of the Arringtons has much of a head for liquor and it wouldn't surprise me in the least if she put up a poor show of it.

"The point is, though, that I'm hot and hungry and bored, and I don't see why we can't play the press gang with our charming hostess and her mammoth husband, and let *them* come watch the sufferers while *we* enjoy a civilized bite to eat!"

"But Cousin Stephen, think how shocking it would be if either of them was to awaken and find an unfamiliar face by the bed."

"The point is that neither of them *will* awaken and what's more," he added virtuously, "it would be much more shocking for either of them to awaken and find our recumbent forms on the floor by their beds, passed out or even dead of hunger. No, really, Cousin, this is too bad. We shall be up all night—you know we shall. Patients *always* spend the night tossing and turning. You've heard all the same sick-nurse stories I have. Why, even the *healthiest* people are bound to be up half the night if there is someone to watch them do it, and there's no denying that neither Perse nor Ramsey has had the sort of day that will encourage a restful night. So come along like a good girl, and let's round up the reinforcements."

There was nothing that Amelia would have liked better than to yield to her cousin's urgings, but perhaps just because of that she felt obliged to raise at least one more demur. She lowered her eyes bashfully and made a confession. "I am ashamed to admit it, but I most sincerely doubt that either my feet or my fortitude will allow me *ever* to put on those horrible sandals again. However, as I have no other footwear with me, I fear that I am confined to my (or, rather, Persephone's) room until my luggage arrives from town."

Stephen greeted this revelation with a shout of laughter which led Amelia to cast a reproachful glance from him to the bed, though the only sign Persephone showed of having heard was to sigh deeply and push her head deeper into her pillow. Obediently stifling his laughter, Stephen strove to reassure his cousin. "As you are being so frank with me, Cousin, I feel constrained to be equally frank and disclose that this would not be the first time, nor yet, I hope, the last, that I have dined with a lady who lacks some article of dress that would be considered *de rigueur* in some circles. I promise, though, that I will endeavor to wrench my mind away from the distracting thought of your bare feet if *you* will consent to ignore the fact that I propose to dine in dusty riding dress. In fine, Cousin," he concluded, "neither one of us would be allowed into Polite Society this evening, so we shall just have to make do with each other."

And then, as he held his hand out to her invitingly, Amelia gave up the fight, and took her cousin's hand in hers. In that manner they were about to leave the room, when a sudden and uncharacteristically conscious look came over Stephen and with an awkward laugh, he dropped her hand and elaborately bowed her out of the room instead.

They wandered downstairs to find that Mrs. Tewks had, for a wonder, anticipated their wishes. She was, she told them virtuously, just about to come upstairs and see if they wouldn't perhaps fancy a bite to eat, as she and Mr. Tewks would be more than happy to sit with the two poor dears, she'd take her affidavit to *that.* And they mustn't worry that she wouldn't know what to do if either should wake up, neither, as she'd plenty of experience sitting with them what was feeling poorly, seeing as how her first husband, Mr. Stevenson as was, had been fearful prone to gout (which was, indeed, what finally killed him) and she had spent many and many a night sitting up with him, with nothing more to do than to fetch him things and duck when his temper got the better of him and he took it into his head to throw things at her.

Stemming this tide of confidences, Stephen assured the landlady that they were extremely grateful for her kind offer, and trusted her implicitly with their friends' well-being, and could dinner be ready in fifteen minutes? Assured that it could be on the table sooner than that, Stephen and Amelia both heaved audible sighs of relief and went back upstairs to freshen up, to the extent that was possible, before dining.

Joining each other in the inn's only private parlor a few moments later, Amelia and Stephen both appeared a bit awkward, only to have the unexpected constraint between them broken by an extremely loud and unmistakable growl from Stephen's stomach. Unable to maintain his gravity, he pointed out merrily that that only proved his point that they were better off out of the sick rooms, and with that, he bowed his cousin to her seat.

To their surprise, the meal was an excellent one. Mrs. Tewks employed none of the arts of French cookery that were so fashionable, but the plain joint which was put down in front of them was well dressed and well cooked, as was every other item on the table. Amelia, who had scarcely eaten at breakfast and had had not so much as a bite since then, applied herself to her plate with such assiduity that it was some moments before she realized that Stephen, having assuaged his own worst pangs of hunger, had laid down his fork and was looking at her with amusement. Blushing, Amelia had started to apologize for her bad manners, but was stopped by her cousin.

"Please, I beg you will not be a goose! Frankly, it is a pleasure to watch you so thoroughly enjoying yourself."

Amelia smiled in return. "I must admit that I have never been one to turn up my nose at my dinner. Indeed," she commented thoughtfully, "I have often suspected that those ladies who make a great show of dainty eating in public frequently gorge themselves at home, since it is clear that no healthy young woman could keep body and soul together on the amount of food that some seem to think it is appropriate to eat in public."

"I believe you're right. And I surmise that it is probably not unlike the men who feel obliged in public to pretend to a great liking for sport, but whom I secretly believe enjoy nothing so much as a quiet nap in a comfortable armchair." Agreeing that fashion was, indeed, an exigent master, they lapsed once again into a companionable silence.

The entrance of Mrs. Tewks's large orange cat provided the next diversion, as the animal strolled over to the table, sniffed about delicately, and then set himself deliberately to licking Amelia's bare toes, which were just peeking out from under her dress. Amelia attempted to appear unconscious of this unwarrantable liberty for some time. Her gravity finally deserted her, however, when Stephen, intrigued as much by the odd faces his cousin was making as by the small noises coming from beneath the table, pushed his chair back and stuck his head under the cloth to discover what was the matter. The serving girl who came to clear the table moments later found the two of them hopelessly convulsed in laughter, his lordship clutching an obviously bewildered cat. Long since convinced that all the gentry were more than a little mad—why else their fascination with the uninteresting question of when the sheets were last laundered?—Molly simply added this to her store of tales of the oddities she had seen, but she did point out to her mother that night that *she* would be that ashamed to be seen carrying on so with a gentleman, with not so much as a man nor woman neither nearby for the sake of what's right and proper.

Needless to say, however, Molly kept her observations to herself, beyond asking if there was anything else she could bring Miss and his Lordship? Assured that Miss and his Lordship were doing quite well, but might fancy a pudding if there were one to be had, Molly had flitted off to the nether regions of the kitchen to determine whether this humble request could be fulfilled. (And that was another thing—maybe that young spark was a lordship and maybe he wasn't, but *she* had always thought that those as were lords and ladies had a better sense of what was due them than to sit down to a meal looking like they'd just jumped out of the saddle, and then to eat whatever they was given like it was what they was used to. His lordship, *if* he was a lordship, was a little too easily pleased for Molly's idea of what a lordship should be.)

Dinner at last being done, Amelia and Stephen regretfully retreated upstairs to find out how the patients were doing. Stephen found Ramsey and Tewks both sleeping soundly, though Tewks was somewhat the noisier about it, and rather than awaken either man simply got himself another chair out of an empty room and joined the slumberers. Amelia, on the other hand, found that Mrs. Tewks had improved her time by knitting at a handsome shawl which she was glad to be able to admire. Mrs. Welton, Mrs. Tewks told her, was beginning to be restless and she (Mrs. Tewks) was very much afraid that Miss Arrington was in for a long night, the sufferer showing signs of becoming feverish and certainly uncomfortable. With surprising kindness, the landlady offered to divide the night with her in order to allow Miss to get some sleep, but Amelia rejected the offer, feeling both that it would be an unwarranted imposition on the landlady and less than kind to Persephone, should she awaken.

That proved to be all too soon, as Mrs. Tewks's predictions were borne out within the hour. Persephone awoke hot, feverish, and still tipsy. She announced her state in a querulous tone that brought Amelia to her feet in an instant, hoping to hush her patient before she awakened the entire house. "Why," Persephone wanted to know loudly and with a pronounced hiccup, "does my *head* ache so, and why does my *leg* ache so, and why does my nose itch?"

For this last question, Amelia could not suggest an answer, but when she reminded Persephone of the day's events as the explanation for at least the first two of her woes, Persephone greeted her explanation with frank disbelief. In fact what she said was, "Are you trying to tell me that I did this to myself just to help that brute of a Peter Ramsey? You're shamming me, and it's not kind. Why, it would have done that beast a world of good to take a tumble, and I don't believe I'd stir a finger to help him if he was to, to, to . . . *How* did you say I hurt myself?"

Patiently, Amelia explained yet again. "You really were quite a heroine, dear. Mr. Ramsey was in great danger, and you leapt to his horse's head to save him." Persephone frowned her disapproval.

"Well, if you're *not* shamming me, then I'm a bigger fool than I thought I was, and ever since I married David Welton, I've known I was quite a fool. Whyever I should have wanted to help that man, I don't guess I'll ever know, but there's no use crying about what's over and done. I do feel like something the cat wouldn't bother to drag in, though."

At this, Amelia smiled, relieved to hear that her cousin could joke, however feebly, at her condition. "The doctor did say you might be feverish tonight, and left a draught for you if you wished it. Do you?"

"I'll confess to you, Cousin, that I've always had an ungodly fear of medicine, ever since I was a little girl and some fool of a doctor gave my father laudanum to help me sleep through some trivial childish ailment and the stuff gave me nightmares. I do feel rather feverish, but all I really fancy is something cool to drink. Have you any barley water?"

"No, but the landlady made up some lemonade just before she retired. You haven't seen her yet, though she watched you for some time while I dined; I think you'll find her a curious soul."

After pouring out Persephone's lemonade, Amelia set about to regale her with the story of their arrival at the inn, hoping to distract her from her aches and pains. In that she had only a mixed success; it was clear from Persephone's occasional grimaces that her leg pained her a great deal, and Amelia guessed that she was, in fact, aching in every limb. Nonetheless, the cool lemonade and Amelia's voice together did seem to soothe her, and she even was able to laugh a bit at the description of Hermione facing down the landlady, although she did say that it was just what she would expect of the girl, that her greatest successes would no doubt always be achieved through her complete lack of consideration for the behavior expected of a lady. The only break in the easy flow of Amelia's narrative came when Persephone asked, without much show of interest, who was caring for the unpleasant Mr. Ramsey. Had Persephone been paying any closer mind, she might have noticed that Amelia's tone became artificially light when she answered that Cousin Stephen had very kindly undertaken that task, and even Persephone noticed that Amelia's account of her dinner with her cousin was delivered with a constraint entirely unlike her normal manner. Unable or unwilling to give the matter much thought in her present condition, Persephone, as it were, filed it away in her mind for consideration at some later date. At this point, she noted merely that it was a curious thing and that she believed that she might, were Amelia to pour her one more glass of the lemonade and shield the candle from her view, fall asleep once again.

This she did. Persephone slept through the rest of the night, only calling out once or twice, and tossing and turning no more than was to be expected after such a day. Amelia, for her part, spent much of the night lost in a thoughtful haze, aware only vaguely of the passage of time and of the distant sound of snores coming from the three sleepers in the next room. It was only as she was watching the dawn break gently over the countryside that she found herself at last falling asleep.

She was roused a few hours later by noises announcing the presence of new arrivals at the inn. Hoping to find that it was the servants for whom they had sent, she twitched her disheveled clothes into some semblance of order, and, grimacing, forced her poor feet into their sandals. Having glanced briefly into the tiny mirror which the room boasted, and having decided that nothing other than a long bath and a complete change of dress was going to allow her to appear even faintly respectable, she tiptoed out of the room and down the stairs. There, much to her surprise, she found not only the servants and baggage, but her father as well.

"Papa! This is delightful, but whatever are you doing here?"

"Hmph! My niece, ain't she? Father's dead, ain't he? Good girl, too. Shouldn't be left alone."

"But, Papa, she was hardly going to be left *alone.* I'm here, as is Cousin Stephen, and now that you've been so kind as to bring Persephone's abigail, I can't imagine that there is a great deal more that she will need from you."

"Company. Comfort. The Good Book. Chess. And you're going back to London."

"That I am not, Papa, and I don't know how you can even think it. It shan't be many weeks that Perse is going to be trapped here, but so long as she is, I'll not be spending my time *frolicking* about Town as if nothing were the matter. Setting aside the fact that you introduced me to my cousins in the first place because I need a female chaperon, I couldn't be so heartless. You know perfectly well that this Season has never meant so much to me as it has to you, and I flatly refuse to go ahead with it as if my best, my only, friend in England were not in distress."

"We'll discuss it."

"We won't."

Hezekiah fumed for a moment, and then exploded. "Just like your mother! Looked a docile little thing, but it wasn't true. Had a mind of her own." And then, to the surprise even of his daughter, who thought she knew him inside and out, Hezekiah wiped a tear from his eye. "That's why I loved her."

Dumbfounded and not knowing what to say, Amelia reached out for her father's hand, but the moment passed as quickly as it had come. "All right. You can stay, but so will I. Better for everyone. You can still get out more, I won't be in that London barn all alone, and my niece and Mr. Ramsey will have some rational company."

Refusing to take offense at this aspersion, Amelia had turned away to seek out Mrs. Tewks, finally locating her in the chicken coop, studying her cocks with a considering eye. Having decided to her own satisfaction the identity of her next victim, she turned her attention at last to Amelia, and exclaimed with annoyance when told that a new guest had arrived at least fifteen minutes earlier and had not yet been properly greeted. Scurrying to the front of the house, she found Hezekiah deeply engaged in conversation with her Tewks. Mr. Tewks was himself of Methodist leanings and the subject of religion had arisen in conversation as Hezekiah's first question to his host was whether there was a Chapel conveniently situated from the inn. Although Mrs. Tewks disapproved of her husband's religious interests, she knew better than to voice her opinions in the presence of a customer whose equipage and tailoring bespoke good money, if simple tastes. While herself more inclined to High Church than Low, Mrs. Tewks was hardly one to set forth her opinion against that of a well-heeled patron, and if Tewks were to find himself on the wrong side of her tongue later that day, well, that was his look-out. Meanwhile, she had the difficult question of how to dispose of her numerous guests to solve, and so she reminded Tewks after shepherding Amelia and her father into a parlor to await their breakfast.

"For where I am to put them all, I'm sure I don't

know!" Mrs. Tewks was busy in the kitchen. She set Molly to tending a calve's foot jelly that she was making up for Mrs. Welton and Mr. Ramsey, while she herself attended the more artful preparations of the kippers, kidneys, and ham that would form the chief part of the breakfast to be served to the healthy members of the party. "Two rooms were all that were needed last night, but we'll need five tonight, not to speak of the servants, and wouldn't you know that they'd come just when I'm in the middle of spring cleaning and with barely a room fit for decent folks. Ah well, life's but a trial and a trouble and so I've often said." And with that philosophical musing, Mrs. Tewks returned her attention to her pots and pans. Her husband, correctly understanding himself to be dismissed, and having no doubt that his wife would solve the seeming problem of where to put this honeyfall of paying customers, quietly absented himself. And if, instead of going out to the stables to make sure the horses were being looked after properly, as his wife assumed, he spent a few minutes with the nabob discussing the troublesome question of whether the presence of stained glass in the church that his wife made him attend would actually endanger his immortal soul, that was, in his opinion, a matter among him, his God, and Mr. Arrington.

Eleven

Peter Ramsey awoke with a groan just as the sun managed to work its way into his room, well into the morning. His memory of the events of the previous day was surprisingly clear, except that he could not, for the life of him, recall receiving a blow to the head that would account for the pounding he was experiencing directly behind his eyes. That his leg should feel like a tiny badger had worked his way into it and was now busy trying to gnaw his way out was only to be expected, but how the animal had got loose in his brain was a mystery. Still, matters could be worse. He'd broken bones before on the hunting field, and knew his powers of recuperation to be good. Although he had heard the doctor expressing some concern as to the full recovery of the leg, he himself felt none. Indeed, had not that blasted Welton woman leapt so officiously to his rescue, he would not have been entirely ill-pleased with his accident.

Having long since come to the conclusion that he was unable to control his ward, he had secretly been considering whether or not there might be some way simply to scotch her first Season entirely; perhaps the mellowing effect of one more year under some better tutelage than she had hitherto received might bring her to some sense. No idea had heretofore presented itself, but he now hoped that his injury might serve as the very excuse for which he had been searching. Obviously, he could not now be expected to accompany Hermione to social engagements—it appeared likely that he would scarcely be walking before the Season was over. And if he decided to retire to his estate in Berkshire rather than face the unpleasant prospect of convalescing in London, could he not also be expected to take Hermione with him? That the girl wouldn't like it, there was no doubt. But perhaps she had already seen enough of the world in the few months she had spent in London to realize that an outright refusal on her part would win the condemnation of numerous people in whose eyes she would wish to appear unobjectionable. She was, after all, young to be out in any event, and there might well be people who would cut her, or as near to it as didn't matter, if she chose to try to appear in Society at a time when her uncle might have been presumed to have had the first call on her attentions. Fortunately, Hermione's frequent complaints about her uncle were taken by many people to have been made in a jesting spirit, and Ramsey believed that Miss Thomason, sensible girl that she was, might well manage to convince his niece that it was in her own best interest to allow that impression to remain. Indeed, if he didn't misjudge his niece's companion, he could imagine her painting a most vivid word-picture of the affecting light in which Hermione would appear were it to become known that she had voluntarily given up her rounds of pleasure in order to nurse her uncle, and hoped that the child's irrepressible urge to self-dramatize might find the image appealing enough to go along with it.

His accident, then, was not without its bright side, and were it not for that Welton woman (and his head),

Ramsey might have been content to view it as an odd but effective bit of Divine intervention. What to do about The Welton was, however, a difficult question. Try as he might, he could not convince himself that he did not owe the creature some considerable gratitude; while convinced in his own mind that he would have done very well without her help, there was no doubt that she must have believed herself to be coming to his aid, and equally little doubt that she had shown extraordinary courage, if very little sense. A man, of course, would have known that it is very nearly impossible to hold a rearing horse, while a truly well-bred woman would never have thought of putting herself forward in that bold manner. But still, if one discounted these facts, there was no denying that it had been a very fine action, of its sort. At the same time, he could scarcely think of a person toward whom he would less have enjoyed feeling grateful. That he had behaved badly toward her only aggravated his chagrin; while hardly a man known for his delicate manners, he had also never before found himself in the equivocal situation of having grossly insulted a lady, if that was what she really was, and then finding himself in her debt. He supposed that at some point, he would have to thank her, and that thought alone would have been enough to make him grimace. The entry of Stephen Arrington into his chamber at that moment, carrying a glass of some foul-looking liquid in his hand, was only the final straw.

"Glad to see you looking so bright and cheery, Ramsey! It's a face to gladden the hearts of your score of well-wishers. Now if you'll only down some of this, you may begin to present an even more sunny countenance to the world!"

"Damn you, Sandston, what the devil are you doing here?"

"Now if that's not gratitude for you! Here I am, worn

virtually to the bone from tending your sickbed (and a nastier snore I don't believe I've ever heard) and you abuse me! I've half a mind to take myself and my secret cures away. *I* don't care if your head bursts open, and Miss Pendergast would probably thank me for it. So if you choose to down a bumper of pure rum and then reject the assistance of the only man in this benighted inn that can help you, that's your business, I'm sure!"

Ramsey frowned. "If you'll stop playing the fool for the moment, I'd be everlastingly grateful. Are you telling me that I was *drunk* last night?"

"As a lord. That's how the sawbones set your leg."

"That explains my head, then. And if I understand correctly that you stayed here during the night to watch me, I am grateful, and if you've got something that will clear my head, I'll be even more so." Ramsey paused, and smiled somewhat ruefully. "I must apologize for my initial greeting. I do seem to get myself off on the wrong footing with your family, but you should understand that I am hardly at my best this morning."

"Lord, I don't hold a grudge, although it does seem hard to be sworn at just when I'm doing one of my rare good deeds. I'm sure my Uncle Hezekiah would draw some Methodistical moral from it, but to me it just seems proof that virtue is not only not its own reward, but is hardly rewarded at all. I'll tell you frankly that I *was* considering reforming, but you've discouraged me. There's no denying it; you have discouraged me."

With that, Stephen cheerfully handed the glass to Ramsey, who downed it in one long gulp. He blanched briefly, opened his eyes a little wider, and then smiled.

"I believe that does help, though I'd not have bet a groat on the possibility that you had no intention of poisoning me. I don't suppose you have any equally efficacious cures for a broken leg?"

"No, I'm sorry, but I haven't nearly as much experience with that. About all I can offer you are the services of your valet, who has just come down from Town, sent here at a run by your underappreciated angel of a ward."

"Angel! Hah! Let me tell you something, Sandston. I'll not pretend that I have much use for you. But I do owe you something, as it appears to me that you have gone out of your way for me in this mess, so I'll tell you for your own good that even if I ever could be brought to consent to your marrying Miss Pendergast, which I could not, you'd regret it before the honeymoon was over. If I were a different sort of man, I'd swear the child was possessed, as several of her governesses have insisted. A nastier, naggier temper I have never seen. I am some years your senior, and believe me, I've known a good number of women, and there were some I'd have matched in a fight against a wild tiger, but I have never met one more ominous than my niece. I owe it to my sister to see the girl well married, but I'll confess to you that there are times, in the dark of the night, when I positively quake at the thought of what I may unleash on some poor, unsuspecting soul who may even, God help him, believe himself in love. You, at least, are simply a fortune hunter; go hunt some tamer prey."

Stephen changed color several times during Ramsey's speech, and then, when he finished, took a deep breath. "It's not true, you know. None of it. Perhaps your niece is no angel, but she is a little darling, and you just don't know enough to see it. And I'm not just hunting for her fortune. I understand that I don't look like a very eligible *parti* at this point, but I hope that when you see that she and I are devoted to each other, you may change your mind. Certainly, I hope you won't try to pressure her into some loveless match just for the sake of *your* pride."

"If you're serious, man, then I'm sorry for it. I can assure you that I will never pressure the girl into anything; I doubt I could even if I wished to. But until she is of age, and that is not for a good many years, she'll not marry without my permission, and I'll not give it for her to marry you. That's all there is to it."

"You think that's all, but it's not, of course. Still, I won't worry you any more about it now. I'll have plenty of opportunity in the next few weeks, for you and my sister are both going to be laid up here for some time. I've no doubt that between us, Miss Pendergast and I will wear you down." With a cheerful grin, and before Ramsey could issue the outraged protest that had sprung to his lips, Stephen whisked himself out of the room. He was replaced shortly thereafter by Ramsey's valet, who did what he could (which was not much) to make his master more comfortable, and who informed him that Hezekiah Arrington was present in the inn, and wished to see him whenever he felt up it. Snapping irritably that he had already been plagued by one unwelcome visitor, and therefore did not understand this sudden solicitude in keeping back a welcome one, Ramsey told his man to ask Mr. Arrington to come on up.

A few minutes later, Hezekiah did so. He walked in and gave a considering glance at his friend. "Look worn to the bone. Not surprising. Would have thought you could handle your own horses, though. And I don't know why you felt obliged to involve my niece in all this."

"Why *I* felt obliged! Hezekiah, this is outside of enough. First that ramshackle nephew of yours makes a dead set at my niece, forcing me to behave in a manner consistent neither with my dignity nor my time, and then your niece plays the heroine at my expense, thrusting herself in where she was neither needed nor wanted! I've great respect for you, as you know, and have considered myself your friend, but I will tell you that if I never see another member of your family again, it will be a good deal too soon for me! And then to have you coming in here and acting as if this matter were of my doing—well, its just too much!"

Hezekiah was unperturbed by this outburst. "Bilious. Not surprising. I'll have my man send up to Town for my liver pills. May help."

"I don't need any liver pills. All I need is an Arrington-free morning."

"Not true. You need the liver pills, and you need the Good Book." With that, Hezekiah sat down and pulled from his pocket a well-thumbed Bible. Ignoring the groan which Ramsey allowed to escape him, Hezekiah opened to the Book of Job, proposing first to read it to Ramsey, and then to discuss with him its meaning and relevance to his current situation. Ramsey's suggestion that he would be better off sleeping than considering theological questions produced no reaction other than a fixed and daunting stare, and with no further delay, Hezekiah began reading. Some minutes later, he was interrupted by a soft knock on the door. Ramsey, clutching for any interruption like a drowning man clutching for straws, called out for the new visitor to enter, only to groan at the discovery that it was Stephen Arrington once again.

Stephen took in the situation at a glance, and laughed out loud. "Uncle, I understand that your religion is more concerned with justice, perhaps, than with mercy, but don't you think that Mr. Ramsey has suffered enough from the one, and deserves some of the other?"

Hezekiah bridled. "Scoff if you like, but no man is ever the worse for hearing the Good Word. Ramsey's no fool, even if you are. Feel better, don't you?" With that, Hezekiah turned to Ramsey for confirmation. The patient, undecided as to whether he would rather be saddled with the nephew or the uncle, cursed his position silently, and decided to walk a middle path. "I do,

Hezekiah, and I thank you for it. You've given me a great deal to think about, but I do feel that I'm getting tired now, and could, perhaps, do with some more sleep. If you would both shut the door on your way out?"

Stephen, seeing through this petty subterfuge, laughed again. "What a pity! And I just came up to tell you that Mrs. Tewks has prepared what looks like a very tempting breakfast for you. But if you're too tired for the Good Book, you must be too tired for food as well."

Ramsey's eyes narrowed. He would remember this.

"Well, perhaps your uncle would be so kind as to continue to read to me for a bit while I eat, and *then* I'll sleep."

"Good idea! I often find that the Word of the Lord aids in digestion. Clears the system along with the head."

And so it came to pass that Peter Ramsey was treated simultaneously to a few mouthfuls of boiled chicken along with a nourishing broth to the accompaniment of a particularly graphic description of boils. He could not fairly be said to have enjoyed the experience, and as Stephen's potion had improved but not entirely cured his head, his rather faint request at the conclusion of the meal that he might be left to himself was heartfelt. Hezekiah, feeling that he had done the sufferer much good, complied, and went off to see if his niece were awake and ready to receive him.

He found Persephone looking even more worn than Ramsey but considerably more pleased to see him. She had been awake for some time, but lacked the strength or will to call out, and had only just been visited by her cousin, who had disappeared back to the kitchen to see if any of the chicken that had been prepared for Mr. Ramsey was available for Mrs. Welton as well. She was, therefore, alone when her uncle knocked softly on the door.

"Uncle! This is delightful. I'd no idea you'd come down, and no doubt should scold you for taking the trouble, except that I'm too glad to see you. It *is* kind."

"Well, Niece, you can hardly think I'd have left you here alone with neither kith nor kin to care for you, except that here-and-thereian brother of yours. I'll tell you frankly that I'd intended to ship Amelia back to Town, but she's dug in her heels and insists that she'll not leave you. Can't say I think the worse of her for it; still, upsets *my* plans. Lesson. Leave the future in the hands of the Lord, and He'll order it as He sees fit, not as you do. Should have known."

Although not doubting for a moment her uncle's sincerity, Persephone could not help but feel that the old gentleman's attitude toward the Lord's intervention partook less of meek acceptance and more of a grudging respect. However, as that was (as he himself would doubtless have pointed out) none of her affair, she did not pursue the question, but instead applied Hezekiah's observation to herself.

"I wish I could tell why the Lord has seen fit to rack me from limb to limb in the service of your friend Mr. Ramsey, but I suppose if I could, the Lord's ways wouldn't be so mysterious after all." Then, seeing a look of some annoyance pass over her uncle's face, she added quickly, "Oh, dear. That did sound like sarcasm, didn't it? And I really did not mean it that way, Uncle, only that I *do* feel awfully low."

Hezekiah softened. "I'm sure you do, child, and I'll not scold you now, but I will tell you that *I,* for one, do see the hand of the Lord in this accident, however unfortunate it seems now. I'll not scruple to tell you that London is even worse than I remember it. I sometimes think all decency has been forgotten! Don't blame *you;* raised to think of nothing but pleasure! But if you use this opportunity to think seriously about your Immortal Soul, you'll be the better for it. You've spent your life among heathens, and its not surprising you're little better than one yourself, but I'd be mortally glad to bring you to the true Word!"

A voice from the doorway saved Persephone from answering. "Papa, this is too bad of you! First, I hear from Cousin Stephen that you've been reading the Book of Job to poor Mr. Ramsey, as if he needed to be depressed any further, and now I hear you delivering a sermon to Cousin Persephone that would be enough to throw her into the Dismals even if she were feeling top of the tree! You came here to help and I will *not* have you take advantage of the situation so shamelessly."

"Amelia, *I* didn't make the situation. The Lord did."

"Well then, let the Lord make the most of it. I'm sure he is capable of doing so without your help!"

Before Hezekiah could reply, his daughter went on. "The first thing that you can do is to go downstairs and explain to Mrs. Tewks that your arrival does not presage the need for slaughtering every animal within a two-mile radius. She appears convinced that so grand a personage as yourself must feast regularly on enormous quantities of flesh and if you don't stop her, we are going to be presented with meals that will not only consume the bulk of your fortune, but will quite deprive you of your appetite just to look at them. *I* tried to tell her, but made no impression at all, being a Mere Female. So *do* go."

Hezekiah appeared to consider this for a moment, then agreed that it might be best if he were to speak to the woman himself. He kissed his niece on the forehead, told her he would be back to see her later, and left the room. Amelia found this meekness a bit surprising, but would have found it less so had she been privileged to hear the conversation between her father and the redoubtable Mrs. Tewks. Hezekiah took care of the matter on which he had been dispatched in little time, simply explaining to the woman that his daughter had been quite accurate in her statement not only that he ate little and simply, but that the very sight of excessive quantities of rich food disturbed his stomach. He then proceeded, however, to discuss with the landlady the state of her soul, and the reasons she had for prohibiting her good husband from following his own conscience. Mrs. Tewks, torn between resentment at this interference and reluctance to offend such a valuable customer, came out much the loser of this discussion, forced to agree to almost everything Hezekiah said. Unfortunately for both Hezekiah and Mr. Tewks, however, Mrs. Tewks's temper was only worsened by her need to keep a civil tongue in her head with the nabob, and her experience with him only strengthened her conviction that the Church of England was the place for her and hers. For the remainder of Hezekiah's connection with The Green Man, Mr. Tewks attended Chapel with his guest; thereafter and evermore, he was to be found (unhappy) in Church.

Meanwhile, however, Persephone was enjoying the respite won for her by Amelia. Her head felt every bit as bad as Ramsey's, but it had not occurred to her brother that she could make good use of the same remedy, perhaps because he had never had occasion to prepare it for a lady. Persephone was forced, therefore, to cope with her swollen head without the assistance of artificial aids, but several glasses of water and a large bowl of soup did a great deal to help her along. Amelia was the most tactful of sick nurses, avoiding entirely the spuriously cheerful talk in which so many seem to feel obliged to engage. She recognized that the greatest kindness she could do her cousin would be to maintain a respectful silence, and did so until Persephone finished the entire bowl of soup, and asked with a bit of a giggle, "Did Uncle *really* read *Job* to Mr. Ramsey? I should like to have seen it."

"Can you for a moment *doubt* it? You know me well enough to know how genuinely I love Papa, but he simply cannot be brought to understand that his religious views are neither widely shared nor very congenial. He honestly believed that he was doing poor Mr. Ramsey a favor, and try as I might, I am quite sure that I will never convince him otherwise. I might add, however, that in this instance he was abetted by your brother, who knew quite well what Mr. Ramsey was thinking. If he is serious about Miss Pendergast, these sorts of tricks will hardly stand him in good stead."

"Oh, but Amelia, he *can't* be serious about that minx, can he? I know I am hardly the one to talk of imprudent matches, but I do know that Stephen could never be happy with that chit. And I'll lay you a pony (or I would, if I had one) that she doesn't care for him any more than she does for a dozen other handsome sparks. She's flattered by his pursuit now, but it doesn't seem to me that she has any real heart in her at all. I probably should be ashamed to say it, knowing what I do now, but I really *did* love Captain Welton when I married him, and I know that I could never worry about myself and my own petty comforts when he was about—*he* was all I could think of, not my carriage or my hair."

"Well, as to that, I can't say, as I never have been in love myself, but I'm not sure it takes everyone the same way." Amelia looked down shyly. "You're so beautiful yourself, that you don't have to worry about how you look, and I would guess that you looked more beautiful than ever when you were in love, just because *everything* you do seems only to make you look more beautiful. But a less handsome girl might give new thought to her face, if she cared what someone else thought about it, mightn't she?"

"Well, I suppose so, but I don't think all of that applies to Miss Pendergast."

"No, of course not. I was just thinking aloud."

Persephone was quiet for a moment. She was neither a stupid nor an insensitive woman, and it struck her that Amelia's comments had very little sound of the hypothetical. Looking back on what she could remember of the last few weeks, she realized that there had been signs aplenty that something was bothering Amelia, and thought ruefully that she should have guessed what that something was most likely to be in a young woman who has just been thrust into Society. But with whom could she have fallen in love? She had seemed to enjoy her dances with several of the men at the balls they'd attended, but Persephone could not think of any one whom it had appeared she favored over the rest, except, of course, Stephen, who had the virtue of familiarity. She had danced twice at her come-out with Jack Dalton, who was a handsome rattle, but surely not the sort to cause any heartburnings in so sensible a woman as Amelia? The Duke of Ainscott had been quite particular in his attentions, but his wit was not keen, and though he was quite a worthy young man, she could not imagine Amelia to have fallen in love with him so quickly, even if it were possible that she could fall in love with a dullard at all. Reviewing the rest of their eligible acquaintances in her mind, Persephone came to the conclusion that there was no one whom she would have thought to have made an impression on Amelia's heart, and, feeling extremely weary, put the puzzle aside for the moment, planning to work on it at a later date and, perhaps, to encourage Amelia to confide in her. Smiling at her cousin, then, Persephone changed the subject and thanked Amelia for her breakfast, and then fell into a sound sleep.

Twelve

Dr. Traherne stopped in briefly to see the two patients in the middle of the morning, and found both to be progressing much as he expected—both were fractious and aching, but neither appeared feverish and he was able to give a reassuring report to the Arringtons. He informed them that the two should still be watched closely for a few days, particularly at night, but that after that, their healing would be largely a matter of time and of rest. He recommended against any thought of moving either for at least three weeks and indicated that he thought it likely, in fact, that it would be at least a month before either could endure the ride back to town.

After the doctor had gone, Amelia retired upstairs to assure herself that Persephone and Ramsey were sleeping, then came back downstairs to find her father and cousin arguing over what was to be done next. It appeared that Stephen had indicated that he intended to take up residence at The Green Man for as long as his sister was immured there, and Hezekiah had objected. As Amelia entered the room, she heard her father declaring that *he* would not stand the nonsense if his nephew chose to ignore the fact that he had perfectly good rooms waiting for him in London and instead decided to pay the doubtless ruinous rates that Mrs. Tewks intended to charge this unexpected party. Stephen replied with some heat that it was exactly what he would expect of his uncle to reduce a matter of family feeling to pounds and pence and Amelia felt it wise to intervene.

"What *is* the matter with the two of you? I feel like a governess who can't leave her charges alone for more than a few moments without one or the other setting up a tantrum! Papa, *your* comments were both rude and unkind, while as for you, Stephen, I should expect you to show more respect for your uncle. I must say, though, that I agree with Papa that you would be best off returning to Town, at least once the doctor has assured us that any danger is past. You'll just fret yourself to flinders here and that will hardly help Persephone. I should think that the best that you can do for her is to visit often with the latest news so that she doesn't feel her absence so much."

"So I'm to be reduced to tale-bearing, am I? I'll have you know, Cousin, that this would not be the first time that I've nursed Perse; when we were children and both had the measles, she was much sicker than I, and I was of considerably more use to her than our lamented father or that fool of a nurse who was supposedly taking care of us, and actually spending most of her time taking care of a bottle of brandy. I don't see why *I* should be banished."

"I've told you; you are to be our ears and eyes in London. I should think that boredom will shortly be our greatest enemy, and I count on you to stave it off."

Hezekiah interrupted. "Won't be bored. *We'll* be here. Just don't want the boy hanging about, getting into trouble." Then, turning directly to Stephen, he added more kindly, "Look here. Didn't mean what I said. Tongue and temper got the better of me. Does you credit to want to stay with your sister, but you know as well as I do that you'll be restless after a few days of it, and we don't need you here kicking up larks. Come visit—not so very far from Town. But don't stay."

Hezekiah seemed to be about to add something, but thought better of it, and instead pursed his lips and looked steadily at Stephen. He, in turn, looked exasperated, but finally shrugged and said, with a laugh, "Since you both seem convinced that I'll be in the way here, I'll return to London as soon as its clear that Perse is on the mend." With that, he turned and stamped out of the room.

Amelia turned to her father. "Papa, I supported you in this because I didn't want to see the two of you fighting, but *why* did you wish Cousin Stephen to leave? I should have thought that you would be pleased at a plan for taking him out of London during the Season, and in any event, that you would at least honor his intentions in wishing to sacrifice his own pleasure to his sister."

Hezekiah was silent for a moment, and then, uncharacteristically, sighed. "I do appreciate it, child. But as much as I may have the interests of my niece and nephew at heart, neither means as much to me as you do, and I'd not see you made any more unhappy, if I can prevent it."

Amelia tried to speak, but found herself tongue-tied for the first time in a lifetime of dealing with her father. He held up his hand, as if to prevent her saying anything. "Think I don't know my own girl? You're in love with the boy, and he don't think any more of you than that you are a much more pleasant relation than he would ever have guessed *I* would provide him. If he comes out regularly to see Persephone, you'll still be seeing more of him than will do your peace of mind any good; you don't need him living here as well."

Finding that she had nothing to say, Amelia simply left the room. She knew that her father was right; indeed, she'd known for weeks that she was falling in love with her charming cousin. She had tried not to be bitter when it became clear that he looked on her in much the same light as his own sister, and even when she heard him talk about Hermione, but she had to admit that there was something in what her father said; she was not certain that her equanimity could survive weeks of living under the same roof as Stephen. The previous evening that they had spent exclusively in each other's company had been in some ways a sore trial to her; she was grateful that it was unlikely to be repeated. She told herself that she had never had any illusions about handsome young men falling in love with her, and that she should be glad that Cousin Stephen so clearly looked on her as a friend, but she found remarkably little comfort in the thought. The quiet life of companionship with her father that had always seemed to her a perfectly pleasant prospect, to be succeeded in later years by the equally pleasant independence that her fortune would bring her, now looked considerably less enticing than once it had, but at least she need not endure Stephen's continual presence as salt in her wound.

When the three gathered for a light luncheon a short time later, it was apparent that Stephen had recovered much of his good temper. As he handed Amelia into the room, he remarked to her in a low tone that, as it appeared that her father would steadfastly oppose his remaining, he supposed that he had best plan on returning to Town, but that nothing that Hezekiah said could keep him from visiting every day. The Season, he said, was probably going to be dull in any event, and would be much the more dull from *her* absence, as well as from that of Persephone. Lest Amelia read too much into this unexpected tribute, however, Stephen had added that Miss Pendergast would almost certainly be found at the inn with some regularity as well, and that *his* visits to Persephone would, therefore, provide him with an entirely unexceptionable means of seeing *her*. Not knowing how to respond, Amelia simply smiled, and spent the meal staring thoughtfully down at her untouched food.

Her father, in contrast, kept up an unaccustomed flow of chatter during the meal. He began by making Stephen an apology which, if grudging by most standards, was quite fulsome for him, and was recognized as such by his nephew. "Nephew, I was out of line this morning; had no business in raising money issues in regard to a family matter. Worried about my niece. Made my temper worse. Point is, though, that I appreciate the fact that you're concerned. Still, I'm right; would be best if you return to your own rooms." He was gratified when his nephew meekly acquiesced and went on from there to a monologue concerning the disastrous effects of government corn policies which was largely incomprehensible to either of his auditors, but served his purpose of preventing other, and more dangerous, conversation.

After lunch, Amelia went up to sit with Persephone, who had awakened with a raging headache and thirst. Assuaging the one with a cool compress to the sufferer's head, and the other with a large glass of Mrs. Tewks's excellent lemonade, Amelia looked briefly about the room to make sure that Persephone's abigail had arranged things properly, and then settled down to spend a quiet afternoon watching the invalid. It was at this point that she first truly appreciated her father's decision to stay with them, for she found that Persephone was fretful and convinced that the *only* thing that could divert her mind from her aches and pains was a game of chess. However, as she was an excellent player and Amelia a hopeless one, their first few efforts ended too quickly to provide any diversion at all, and Amelia called for her father to salvage her cousin's temper and her own pride.

Hezekiah was agreeable to his task; he had enjoyed several games of chess with his niece in Town, and had been surprised to find that she was more likely than not to beat him. Indeed, he had asked her at one point how it came about that she played so very well, and she had informed him that one of her early governesses had been a truly superior player. The woman had been so pleased to find a natural pupil in Persephone that she had spent hours passing on her skills, time which could, perhaps, have been better spent on some more practical field of learning, but for which Persephone nevertheless remained grateful. When, some years later, she had attended school with Anna Milbanke, her skills had been further honed, as that remarkable young lady had shared Persephone's passion for the game, bringing to bear upon it her rare mathematical ability. (When Anna had married Lord Byron shortly after leaving school, Persephone had wondered whether the poet had fully appreciated his wife's skills. Her skepticism had increased when her father repeated to her Caroline Lamb's cruel remark that Byron would never stay with any woman who had a poor figure, went punctually to Church, and understood statistics, and was confirmed when she heard of Anna's separation from her husband after only one year of marriage. Persephone had renewed her acquaintanceship with the baroness following Captain Welton's death, and continued in recent months to play regularly with, and to be beaten regularly by, her.)

This afternoon, Persephone's game could not be said to be at its best, but even so, her uncle found himself hard put to avoid a number of clever traps, escaping only narrowly from being mated after only ten moves, and eventually winning only because Persephone's discomfort prevented her from paying close attention to her endgame. Still, the game served to distract her for several hours from her multitudinous aches and pains, and she was grateful. By the time Uncle Hezekiah left her room, she was ready for sleep, and between chess and napping, passed a not unpleasant afternoon.

Peter Ramsey was less fortunate. He had awakened shortly after Persephone and heard the voices of Amelia and Persephone as they spoke softly in the next room. He heard Amelia call down the stairs for some lemonade to be sent up for Mrs. Welton, and longed for some cooling drink himself, but was reluctant to shout out for assistance. He disliked feeling dependent and was particularly reluctant to increase his indebtedness toward any member of the Arrington family, toward whom he felt, by this time, a universal hostility. While he had no one to care for him with quite the concern with which Persephone was being watched, he assumed that George, his valet, would be up shortly and that he could then command the man to bring him whatever he pleased, but in this, he was mistaken.

George, having seen his master dead to the world, had decided to spend the afternoon improving his acquaintance with young Molly, who had served him his breakfast shortly after his arrival and had intimated that she was not averse to spending her free afternoon, which happened to be that very day, with a handsome gentleman from London. Thus, at the very moment Ramsey decided to break down and shout for George, George was to be found in a scenic and secluded stand of oak trees overlooking Farmer Robinson's cow pasture, ardently describing to a fascinated Molly the complexities of dressing a swell like Mr. Ramsey, at the same time he was attempting to perform the opposite task for Molly herself. (In this, George was unsuccessful. Molly had not arrived at her twenty years without having achieved some knowledge of the male animal and suspected quite rightly that she would see considerably more of Mr. George in the future if he saw a bit less of her in these early days of their friendship. Molly had been thinking for some months that it was time and enough for her to be settling down and believed that marriage to a valet in a fashionable London house might be just the thing. That she found George himself to be rather appealing was an unexpected but not unappreciated bonus.) Thus, Ramsey's call for George was not answered by the valet but by Stephen, who lounged into the room, unmistakably amused at Ramsey's look of dismay.

"Always pleased to see your smiling face, as well, Ramsey. What is it you need? That man of yours has wandered out to try his hand with the local belle, and much luck I wish him! I'd send my uncle in here to amuse you with some more delightful Biblical passages—I thought of suggesting Revelations to him for his next effort—but he's busy attempting to save his King from my sister. My cousin is taking some much needed rest, and neither Miss Thomason nor your niece has returned from Town, so you and I are the last two souls simultaneously awake and with nothing to occupy ourselves in this entire blasted inn. *I'd* be happy to read to you if you like, but as I have discovered no reading matter in the inn other than my uncle's Bible, and I defer to him as a reader of *that* work, I thought I might instead discuss with you the ways in which you have thoroughly mishandled and misjudged Miss Pendergast."

And that, over Ramsey's loud objections, was exactly what he proceeded to do, pausing only long enough to call downstairs to Mrs. Tewks that some ale was needed by the invalid and his devoted nurse. Settled down comfortably in the chair in which he had passed the previous night, ale tankard in hand, Stephen entered into a monologue that drew some reluctant admiration from his auditor for its fluency and audacity, if for nothing else. By the time Ramsey was permitted to interject so much as a word, he had heard that it was not remarkable that he had been thrown by his horse, as it was obvious that he hadn't the least idea how to handle spirited young animals. What you *didn't* do, Stephen informed him severely, was tug and pull at them, reminding them every moment that they are being ridden, and ridden hard. Instead, you employed the lightest of hands on the bridle, only keeping yourself in readiness to pull up if the delightful creature should get just the *smallest bit* out of hand.

"A metaphor, you see, my good Ramsey, and quite a clever one, *I* think. You've been riding Miss Pendergast like a cart horse, when in fact and as should be obvious to even the meanest intelligence, which I believe yours ain't, she's the purest thoroughbred. *Of course* she kicks up larks. You have practically *invited* her to do so, with your prosing and your scolding. Why, if she were a boy, she'd have run away to sea by now, just to show that she's got some spirit left that you haven't entirely *crushed* out of her."

"The metaphor, Sandston, has the virtue neither of originality nor accuracy. Hermione is not a thoroughbred; she's a rogue, and if she were a boy, she'd be carted home every night by the Watch, I've no doubt, having engaged in every form of destructive mischief. You think I don't understand the girl, but I do. She doesn't have high spirits; she just can't bear to be crossed. Now your sister has 'high spirits,' if by that you mean that she's a spirited girl with some daring and style. You noticed that it was she, and not my ward, who leapt for my horse's bridle yesterday. I'm not saying that I admire the action. It was a damn waste of time. But still, *that's* the sort of thing I'd call spirited, and not simple bad manners and flaunting behavior, which is all my niece knows. Damn it, Sandston! You've been out in Society long enough to know how ladies of quality behave; if you'd never seen it before, you saw it in your cousin at your cousin's ball. Surely you can see the difference between her and my niece? I'm not saying that it's entirely the girl's fault; she wasn't raised well, and she sadly feels the want of her mother. But that doesn't change what she is *now,* and that is a hazard and a terror, and if I *didn't* keep a firm hand on the bridle, to return to your rather hackneyed metaphor, she'd bolt in a minute, just as that ill-conditioned beast of mine did yesterday when I was so foolish as to withdraw my attention from him for a moment."

Stephen mulled over this speech for a moment, sipping delicately at his ale, and then said musingly, "Perse and my cousin are a pair, ain't they, though? Of course with Perse, you see it the minute you look at her. She may be my sister; in fact, of course, she *is* my sister. But that don't change the fact that she's a damned handsome girl *and* a good one as well. Don't you fool yourself, Ramsey. Perse looks a lady because she is one, and a finer one *I've* never known. Lord knows she was a fool to marry David Welton, and I was a fool to let her, but she's young, and it was an easy mistake to make. He *looked* a gentleman, did our Captain Welton, and was seen with the best. How was an innocent girl like Perse to know any different?"

Stephen seemed to await an answer to this question but as none was, not surprisingly, forthcoming, he went on. He neither knew nor, probably, would much have cared that his words were largely unattended. Ramsey was too busy musing on Sandston's remarks about his sister. One would expect, of course, that a man would speak well of his own sister, for his own credit if nothing else. But this accolade sounded more sincere than perfunctory, and added to Ramsey's growing feeling that he had made a serious mistake about the blasted Widow! Meanwhile, however, Stephen went on.

"Funny thing is, though, that Cousin Amelia's as good a gal as Perse is, though you *wouldn't* know it to look at her, and where she got it from escapes me. She never learned her manners from my uncle; it's my belief that he's queer in his attic. And I'm not just talking about religion, mind you, though that's queer enough. I mean to say, religion is all well and good, and I myself should probably not like to get along without it; the Season is exhausting as it is, and I shudder to think what it would be like if people felt free to hold routs on Sundays. Still, when it comes to reading nothing but the Bible and refusing to dance or play at cards or smoke and to believing (and, what is worse, *saying*) that it's off to the fire and brimstone for those souls who do, well, it's outside of enough! And that ain't all that's odd about Uncle Hezekiah, not by a great deal. He's got more blunt than the Treasury, but still insists on going to his office every day like some damned clerk, and going there *on foot,* as if he couldn't afford a *dozen* coaches, and he's got some ideas about free trade and reforming Parliament that don't bear looking into any too close. Why, it wouldn't surprise me in the least if he were a *Whig,* as if the Arringtons hadn't been Tory since before the Flood. Well, I ask you! Is it likely that Amelia learned to be such a right 'un from him? Must have come from her mother's family, although *that* don't seem in the cards either, what with their being little better than heathen, so far as I can tell. All in all, it's a remarkable thing, don't you think?"

As both men had punctuated their conversation by steady pulls on their second tankards of ale, brought up by a thoughtful Mrs. Tewks, and as the afternoon was rather a warm one, it was perhaps not surprising that the only answer Stephen got was a loud snore. Stephen considered awakening Ramsey to continue their discussion, but felt that he was unlikely to make any further progress in correcting the man's misapprehensions about his niece's character at this point, and tiptoed out of the room, having first thoughtfully drawn the shades so that the afternoon sun should not shine into the sleeper's eyes. Looking in briefly at his sister, he found that she, too, had drifted into sleep, having completed her game with her uncle, and he went off to see what other amusement The Green Man might hold for him.

Stephen found his cousin Amelia out in the garden behind the inn. It was too early in the year for many flowers to be in bloom, but the trees were beginning to show green, and there was a promise of early crocus and daffodil in the beds, scattered among the more homely signs of Mrs. Tewks vegetables. Amelia had discovered a small bench under one of the oaks; during the heat of summer, it would be in full shade, but now, on this early spring day, it enjoyed a dappled sunlight that played about her figure, casting light on her lustrous black hair, and a becoming shadow on her face. She had a small sketchbook on her lap, and was so deeply engaged in attempting to catch the lights and shades of the budding garden that she didn't notice her cousin's arrival until his own shadow fell across her page.

Amelia started in surprise, scattering the pens which she had laid carefully on her outspread skirt so that they should be within easy reach. Laughing, she and Stephen bent to recover them, and then Stephen, over her protests, took the sketchbook and began leafing idly through its pages.

After a few moments of silence, he turned to her with a look of mock outrage on his handsome face, and exclaimed, "Cousin, if this isn't the greatest hoax! You cannot deny that the evening we met, you intentionally impersonated a creature of no talent whatsoever. Why, you as good as declared that anyone foolish enough to marry you would be entering into a virtual domestic desert. Now I discover that you not only draw, as I suppose all young ladies of fashion are required to do, but do so exquisitely. Why have you never shown off any of your work? I'm sure these are better than half the things the Academy displays."

"Don't be absurd. I confess that I do like to draw; I believe that it is my *only* talent, if it is one. But I've never had any patience with girls, or more often their doting mothers, who drag out insipid watercolors or charcoal sketches that enjoy neither originality nor even simple accuracy for the enforced admiration of unoffending friends and relations. My art, such as it is, is only for my own amusement."

"Now it is you who are absurd, Cousin. It is like you, I know, to undervalue yourself, but it really is too unfair of you to have kept these accomplishments so secret. *I've* no artistic ability whatsoever, but I do like good art, and should dearly have loved to have seen these before. You must at least promise to share them with Perse during her convalescence; *she* does have some small amount of facility, although nothing like your own, and perhaps you can draw with her while she is confined to her chair." As Amelia refused to catch his eye, Stephen took her hand. "Promise me."

Amelia laughed. "Of course, if you think Persephone would enjoy that. Indeed, next time you go to Town, you could bring back my paintbox. The housekeeper will know where it is kept, and if the weather stays fine, we might even set up an easel out here for Persephone to work at. I'd be more than glad to show her whatever few tricks *I* know, though I'm sure you're making too much of my efforts."

"That's as may be, but I can assure you that Perse will be delighted at the prospect of working with you, once we've shown her what you can do. Why, if you can pass on one-tenth of your skill to her, she may consider her injury in the light of a blessing!"

Stephen and Amelia wiled away the rest of the pleasant afternoon in the garden, each admiring thc fineness of the day and the wit of a good companion, as Amelia completed her drawing. Dinner in Hezekiah's presence was a subdued affair compared to the intimate meal of the night before, and Amelia spent the balance of the evening in Persephone's room, reading quietly to her. Ramsey only woke briefly enough to enjoy a small supper, and long before midnight, sleep had overtaken every one of the inhabitants of The Green Man.

Thirteen

The next morning was similarly uneventful. The two invalids had passed a quiet night, each awakening only a few times, needing cooling draughts. Trays were brought up to them and to the Arringtons and Lord Sandston, each of whom had breakfasted separately, at different times, in their own rooms. After an early tea, Amelia once again retired to the garden and had been joined by Stephen when they heard the sound of a carriage pulling into the yard of The Green Man. Guessing correctly that this would be Miss Pendergast and Miss Thomason, they had hurried around to the front of the inn, arriving in time to see Tewks handing Miss Pendergast down with as much gentleness as if she were a piece of fine china. Miss Thomason was handed down next with more efficiency but less tender care.

Amelia found it difficult to maintain her smile as she saw the glowing look with which her cousin greeted Miss Pendergast, although she did take some comfort in the rather offhand response he received. Hermione, in fact, felt herself to have been rather put upon, and was not enjoying charitable emotions toward *any* of the players in the drama, including Lord Sandston. As selfish as she was, even she would have been hard pressed to put into words precisely who or what it was that had slighted her, but there is no doubt that slighted, she felt, she had been. She couldn't exactly *blame* his lordship for having remained with her uncle; Rachel had actually succeeded in making her understand that it had, in fact, been both generous and proper of him to have done so. Still, she couldn't avoid feeling that everyone else was having all the *fun;* to have camped out in a country inn without so much as an abigail to inhibit her was just the sort of adventure to appeal to her hoydenish soul, and while it had not occurred to her two days earlier to volunteer to act as a nurse, it seemed to her that the others had conspired to arrange matters to *their,* but not to *her,* satisfaction.

First her carriage had been *impressed* as a *hospital cart;* then she had been *marched* down dusty roads to this obscure hostelry; *then* she had been *forced* to take matters into her own hands so that The Woman would so much as allow them to enter her loathsome little establishment; and *then* she had been bundled off to Town to perform other people's errands like little more than a *servant.* Lord Sandston might protest his devotion to her all he liked; she was quite certain that none of the other swains who ardently pursued her would have so readily dispatched her in so highhanded a manner. He was certainly very handsome, and quite the most amusing man she had yet encountered, but he would have to learn that she could not be treated lightly.

Thus it was that Hermione returned Stephen's effusive salutation with a cool nod, and a casually extended hand. In contrast, Rachel's greeting was all warmth. After receiving a comfortable report on the progress of the patients ("Ramsey's sleeping off his lunch, and Perse is, I believe, plotting her revenge upon my uncle for a drubbing she took from him yesterday in chess."), she expressed her sympathy for the difficult nights which, she was quite sure, had been passed by Miss Arrington and Lord Sandston. When Stephen described quite graphically the sights and sounds of Ramsey's sickroom on the night of the accident, complete with an uncanny imitation of the rather distinctive noises that issued from Tewks's nose, Rachel at first attempted to stifle, and then gave way to, gales of laughter. Hermione, however, perceptibly tilted up her little nose and remarked that she had never found the antics of rustics to be particularly amusing. This pronouncement drew surprised stares from all three members of her audience, and a sharp rebuke from Rachel as being neither polite nor original as the identical comment had been made by a guest of Mr. Ramsey's some evenings before. Hermione stamped off in a huff.

While Amelia was reluctant to comment on Hermione's behavior, Rachel decided that their joint adventure had rendered the Arringtons in some sort family, and felt no such qualms. She had been longing to unburden herself to someone for two days, Hermione's behavior having been quite intolerable from the moment they had entered the carriage to return to London. Stephen thus found himself subjected to the second comprehensive denunciation of Hermione Pendergast in two days by one of Miss Pendergast's relatives. While it would be too much to say that he was convinced by Miss Thomason, any more than he had been by Ramsey, that Hermione was the devil incarnate, there is no denying that he was somewhat shaken in his infatuation. His protestations to Ramsey and to Persephone had been entirely truthful; having been anxious initially to meet the heiress solely out of a desire to ease his family's financial woes, he was now genuinely taken with her. He was not, he thought, blind to her faults, but honestly believed them to have been caused by the mistreatment that she was suffering at the hands of her guardian. In his eyes, the *real* Hermione was open and confiding, headstrong but not ill-natured, and totally charming.

Despite his polish, Stephen was, after all, quite a young man, and a surprisingly guileless one; he had taken Hermione largely as she presented herself. Gradually during the course of the past few weeks, and even more since the evening at Almack's, his lordship had built up for himself an image of Hermione as little less than a fairy princess, to be rescued from her wicked uncle; the fact that he found the wicked uncle to be an exceedingly congenial companion, and that Miss Thomason, for whom he had a great deal of respect, seemed to share Ramsey's opinion of Hermione, could not help but cloud that image. He was not yet ready to join in condemnations of the girl, but was prepared to admit that she could, perhaps, be a bit trying if not given her own way.

Rachel, it transpired, had not yet taken her tea, and she, Amelia, and Stephen therefore repaired immediately to Mrs. Tewks's parlor to rectify the situation. There they found Hermione and Hezekiah sitting in glum silence, looking at each other as if they were strange animals in a menagerie. Hermione had flounced into the room only a few minutes earlier, secretly hoping to find Tewks and to repeat her previous triumphs with that uncritical gentleman. (Hermione's comment to Stephen had not only been, as Rachel pointed out, unoriginal, but extremely misleading as well, giving as it did the impression that Hermione felt herself above "rustics." In fact, one of her sole genuine virtues was that she was no snob; she was inconsiderate to her own servants only because she was inconsiderate to *everyone,* but she rarely felt herself above her company, and generally was perfectly content to pass the time of day with anyone who was inclined to admire her.) Finding instead that Mr. Arrington had taken up residence in the parlor to enjoy one of his few indulgences, an afternoon cup of Indian tea, she had attempted to withdraw. Hezekiah, however, believed it his duty and that of every creature who had been saved to attempt to bring to salvation such of the young as were straying from the paths of righteousness, and had called Hermione back into the room and proceeded to lecture her on the general impropriety of her behavior. Pointing out in as kind a manner as he could that her headstrong and thoughtless ways were the ways of Satan and that true Beauty was to be found only on the Lord's Pathways, he had urged her to pray briefly with him that she might see the light of the Lord and turn her back on the darkness of the Devil.

When that cheerful young pagan had simply stared at him, aghast, he became somewhat more stern, beginning to describe in some detail the likely end of a creature such as herself, given over solely to the Pleasures of the Flesh and ignoring the Call of the Spirit. Hermione succeeded in interrupting this litany only by blurting out that she was quite sure her uncle would not approve of her listening to such talk, as he was quite strict about her attending Church every Sunday. She greeted Stephen's entrance, then, with a delight that was unfeigned and did much to restore to him his previous opinion.

Like Rachel, Hermione was extremely hungry, and Stephen disappeared swiftly into the kitchen to cajole a meal for the two girls out of Mrs. Tewks. He failed to find her, but found instead that Molly had returned from another walk with George and was more than happy to serve a substantial tea to the ladies. She was feeling quite cheery, convinced that she and Mr. George would deal together famously once he recovered from his chagrin at her unexpected virtue, and had decided that it was quite a lark to have such a large party at the inn. She had been upstairs to see if anything was needed, and believed that she had never seen such a beautiful lady as that Mrs. Welton as had hurt herself so bad, while it was not in her nature to object to any party that included several handsome gentlemen as well. All in all, life was looking particularly appealing to Molly, and far from grudging the extra work she almost bounced into the parlor with her laden tray moments after Stephen returned to his companions, deftly laying out a tempting array of meats, fruits, and sweetmeats. The display was, indeed, so attractive that Stephen and Amelia declared that they both needed fortifying after their exertions in caring for the sick, and shamelessly indulged in a second tea, while even Hezekiah found himself nibbling at some fruit, although it was hardly his practice, as he said, thus to gratify the flesh.

After the completion of a merry meal, Rachel announced her intention of going upstairs to sit with Persephone, and Hezekiah said that he would do the same with Ramsey. Hermione, casting a meaningful look at Stephen, said that she should love to see the pretty little stream of which she had caught a glimpse from the carriage. Stephen felt guilty about thus abandoning his cousin, but his desire to be alone with Hermione defeated his conscience, and the two set off together, to Hezekiah's silent but patent disapproval. Amelia, avoiding her parent's eye, stated her plan to return to the garden to complete the drawing that she had begun that morning, and the party thus dispersed.

Rachel found Persephone once again awake, and once again thirsty, but otherwise feeling better. She procured her some tea from the cooperative Molly, and settled down for what she called a comfortable cose. In fact, as old friends so often will, the two drifted into tales of their schooldays, and soon gusts of laughter could be heard issuing from the invalid's room. Ramsey, similarly awake and talking politics with Hezekiah, tried unsuccessfully to suppress a pang of jealousy. The Corn Laws were fascinating, and Hezekiah Arrington's opinions on issues of trade were always of interest, but it *did* sound as if Miss Thomason and The Welton were having considerably more fun than he was. Hezekiah couldn't help noticing that Ramsey's eyes seemed repeatedly to stray toward the other room, and remarked irascibly that even such sensible women as Miss Thomason and his niece could scarcely be relied upon to conduct a rational conversation without engaging in this sort of racket. Ramsey agreed weakly and attempted to concentrate his attention on Hezekiah's analysis of the significance of the recent reform riots in the North but was frankly relieved when Rachel poked her head into the room.

"Mr. Arrington, your niece requests . . ." she turned to hear Persephone's faint words, "No, *demands* a rematch. She claims that you took the most *base* advantage of her yesterday."

Hezekiah smiled, but replied that he could not possibly abandon his companion when Ramsey suggested that Hezekiah might, with the assistance of Tewks, carry him into Mrs. Welton's room and put him in an armchair with his leg raised, so that he might watch their game. He felt that his next meeting with the widow was inevitably going to be an extremely awkward one. However, he was never one to shy at fences, and thought he'd best get it over with quickly and with as many other people present as he could arrange so as to minimize the possibility of an actual shouting match. Hezekiah agreed with the plan and went off in search of the landlord.

By the time the two men returned, Rachel and Molly had set up everything that was needed in Persephone's room which was, fortunately, a large one. Having raided some of the empty rooms in the inn, Rachel had found two comfortable armchairs for the invalids; two smaller chairs for them to rest their legs upon; two additional chairs for herself and Mr. Arrington, and a small deal table, upon which she had set out the chess pieces. Hezekiah viewed her arrangements with approbation, and asked her to help him move his niece, something they accomplished quite handily together.

"Good strong girl. Like to see that. Healthy," had been his comment before removing to Ramsey's room with Tewks. His transfer was accomplished with equal facility, due largely to the landlord's enormous strength, and Ramsey found himself confronting Persephone Welton for the first time since the accident.

They looked at each other in silence for a moment, and then Ramsey nodded his head in the closest approach to a bow he could manage in his circumstances. "Although I can remember almost nothing of yesterday's events, Ma'am, I'm reliably informed that I stand, or rather sit, considerably in your debt. I believe that the last time we spoke, I had occasion to give you some offense. As it appears likely that we will be spending some considerable time in this inn together, do you think that you might see fit to view my present discomforture as Divine Retribution, and offer me human forgiveness for my transgression?"

Hezekiah frowned at this speech, but Persephone (recognizing as Ramsey had that they would inevitably be thrown together) reluctantly smiled and replied with rather a cold dignity that she believed that they would both do best to forget that there had been any grounds for offense. She felt that she could say no more in the presence of Rachel and her uncle, but it had, in fact, already occurred to her that Mr. Ramsey's assumptions about her were not really so unreasonable, given his knowledge of her husband, and that in turning her fury on him, she was really blaming him for Captain Welton's misdeeds. It was not, after all, his fault that her husband had been an unprincipled wretch, nor was he to be blamed for assuming that she was privy to Welton's goings-on or that, had she been so, she would look with equal favor on even less seemly activities. She still believed that any friend of Captain Welton's was likely to be a wastrel and a sot, but acknowledged that those characteristics, if Mr. Ramsey had them, were unlikely to manifest themselves while he was tied to a sick bed. In any event she had no more desire than did Ramsey to pass the coming weeks in either sullen silence or a raging feud and had already determined that if an apology were offered her, she would accept it. Indeed, it had partly been in the hope that Ramsey would offer to join them that she had sent Rachel on her errand into his room. With the issue of their reconciliation out of the way, then, she prepared to challenge her uncle.

The afternoon passed quietly and pleasantly. Rachel, who scarcely knew a pawn from a knight, had brought with her some fine embroidery, and sat sewing, looking up only occasionally as some comment was made by one of the players or by Ramsey, who, when he found that neither Persephone nor Hezekiah was the sort of player who demanded total silence, interspersed numerous questions and comments with the moves. He was, himself, a fair player, and shared with most men the assumption that the game was too complex and mathematical for a woman to play well. He was startled, then, to find that Persephone's play was not simply good, but elegant, and that Hezekiah, also a fine player, spent the entire match on the defensive, finally losing decisively as Persephone passed a pawn and created her second Queen. Hezekiah, recognizing his fate, conceded the game gracefully, and Rachel, tidying up her threads, announced that the afternoon was now far advanced and that it was nearly time for her and Hermione to return to Town if they didn't want to travel in pitch darkness. She and Hezekiah, then, reversed their earlier procedure. Working together again, they returned Persephone to her bed and then Hezekiah set out to look for Tewks while Rachel returned the various tables and chairs to the rooms from which she had taken them.

Persephone and Ramsey, left alone for a few minutes, were silent until Persephone said, "I couldn't say very much to you earlier, as I believe that my uncle, thankfully, does not know much about my late husband, and without knowing the story of his goings-on there was certainly no way to make him understand *your* behavior. But I did want to tell you that I have given the matter some thought. You must understand that it has been difficult enough to deal with my widowhood and my straitened circumstances; the shock of learning that perhaps the only thing that Captain Welton *did* leave me was a tainted reputation was too much for my temper. Your error was, I believe, all too easily explained."

Ramsey, recognizing the apology as a handsome one, wished to be equally conciliatory, but his judgment was not equal to his desire. Persephone, who had been smiling ruefully, stiffened when Ramsey replied the reputation of her father and brother were such that he had been perhaps too ready to believe that she was less than fastidious, and the warmth in her voice turned to ice. "David Welton, who was, I believe, *your* friend, appears to have been no gentleman; my brother, in contrast, is. If you believe yourself to be complimenting me by comparing me favorably with him, you are much mistaken. Indeed, Mr. Ramsey, I find that you are *frequently* mistaken, as much in your judgment of horses as of people. What *could* have possessed you to ride a beast that you couldn't handle, endangering yourself and everyone you met?"

Ramsey, justifiably proud of his horsemanship, stiffened in his turn. "There was nothing wrong either with my horse or my handling! From your foolish behavior, it was all too obvious that you know nothing about horses, or you would know that anyone may have an occasional mishap. However, the only *danger* was that which you created with your ill-judged leap to my animal's head. Had you not interfered, I'd have had him under control soon enough."

"*What?* Without the use of your leg?"

"Without the use of my leg. My only problem was in keeping the creature from trampling *you*!" Ramsey knew quite well that he was speaking sheer nonsense, but he was too angry to care. Why he ever should have wished to make up to this woman, he couldn't think, but he was quite certain he would not repeat his error. She was a shrew and a harridan, and probably, for all her high-sounding protestations, no better than she should be!

Thus, by the time Hezekiah and Rachel returned to Persephone's room, the fragile harmony had been shattered. Those two were not, of course, to know what had passed during their absence, but even Hezekiah, not notably sensitive to atmosphere, remarked to Rachel as he handed her downstairs that it seemed to him that Ramsey and his niece were not on the best of terms. Rachel agreed, but was unable to enlighten Hezekiah as to the reasons for their mutual antagonism, commenting only that it did seem rather a shame, as there was no way for them entirely to avoid each other's company during their convalescence.

It was, by now, quite late in the afternoon and the spring sun, while surprisingly strong at midday, was already giving way to the night. Amelia had long since come inside, it having become too chilly to draw in the garden, and was sitting musing in the parlor when, at almost the same moment, Hezekiah entered with Rachel on his arm and Stephen with Hermione on his. The animation in Stephen's face hit Amelia like a blow, but she bore it with her usual grace. Rachel and Hermione said their farewells and Hezekiah and Stephen went up to their rooms to dress for dinner while Amelia went off to find Mrs. Tewks and to make arrangements for trays to be brought up to Persephone and Ramsey. Dinner was another subdued affair, and a pall seemed to fall over the threesome as the meal progressed. At the conclusion of the meal Stephen announced that, as Perse appeared to be coming along prosperously, he would return to Town the next day to perform any commissions that were needed, and the three retired to their respective rooms for the night. That sleep still eluded each of them was, they were convinced, due simply to the discomforts of unfamiliar beds.

Fourteen

Stephen awakened at an unusually early hour the next morning and spent some time lying in his bed, thinking lazily about Hermione. Whatever her relatives might think, she was a charming child. It was a shame, of course, that she was so *very* accustomed to having her own way; perhaps she could spend more time around his cousin Amelia, and see what could be accomplished with a gentle manner. Indeed, it seemed to him that Hermione would benefit greatly from more exposure to his cousin. While she probably did not share Amelia's native talent, it would be a very pleasant thing if she could learn some of her artistic facility. Amelia's own was truly remarkable. Stephen had actually done himself less than justice when he said that he lacked aptitude. In fact, his drawing was quite good. Still, it was nothing as compared to Amelia's and hers was a gift which he greatly admired. While thinking about Amelia, he realized that there was little about her that he did *not* admire, from her sound good sense to her quiet voice. It was a pity, of course, that she was not handsome, but when one knew her better, neither was she so very plain. Yes, Stephen thought to himself, when I've married Hermione I will try to be sure that

Amelia is often a guest in our home. *Her* example should give Hermione just the added polish that she needs.

(In London, Hermione was sound asleep as Stephen made these plans for her future. However, had she been aware of them, she would have squeaked in protest. *She* did *not* particularly care for Amelia, whom she had dubbed fubsy-faced and nearly as Methodistical as her *very* peculiar father and she found paintings boring to look at and tedious to execute. Furthermore, she would have been outraged at the very idea that there was anything she needed to achieve perfection in Stephen's eyes. Her views on love, had she bothered to state them, were that it should be complete, wholehearted, and entirely blind to fault. Not, of course, that she *had* any faults, but if she *did,* she did *not* expect her lover to be aware of them.)

(Amelia, too, slept, dreaming of Stephen. Persephone dreamed of David Welton, and awoke in a cold sweat.)

By nine o'clock, the inn was stirring. Hezekiah had breakfasted some hours before and was out on a morning constitutional, a daily ritual which he sincerely despised but was recommended by his medical man as a relief from the cares of his busy life. George could be found in the kitchen chatting with the fascinating Molly while she prepared a tray for him to bring up to his master who had awakened, he confided to Molly, in a vile mood, swearing at his leg, his valet, and the world in general. Persephone's abigail, feeling injured at George's obvious preference for the rustic Molly, had already taken breakfast up to her mistress and was about to return to get another tray for Amelia, who had decided to keep her cousin company over her meal. (This, too, was an injury in the abigail's mind. Why should *she* be expected to serve Miss Arrington? A pleasant-enough young lady, no doubt, but not *her* young lady.) Stephen, too, having decided to get out of his bed, determined to join Amelia and Perse over a small breakfast, and ran down the stairs quickly to ask Molly if she could oblige him. She did so willingly, and a merry party soon formed in Persephone's chamber.

Breakfast was scarcely complete when Hermione and Rachel arrived once again at the inn, bringing with them this time numerous books to amuse both invalids, as well as some fashion magazines specially for Persephone. They also brought a message for Hezekiah from his chief clerk, the man having arrived at their doorstep early that morning with an inquiry as to whether they were likely to see his employer that day. Upon hearing that Hezekiah was out walking, Rachel volunteered to go find him, as she was the only ambulatory member of the party who had not yet had the opportunity to explore the environs of the inn. Stephen announced his intention of returning to Town almost immediately, and Hermione suddenly recalled that she had forgotten to cancel an appointment in the early part of the afternoon which it would be simply *too* bad of her to miss. Hezekiah and Rachel returning to the inn just as Hermione made this announcement, Rachel stated that she, for one, had absolutely no intention of getting right back into their carriage, and that Hermione would simply have to send one of the servants back to Town to cancel her engagement. Just as Hermione was beginning to pout, however, Hezekiah surprised them all by saying that the message from his clerk made it imperative that he return to London that afternoon but that as there was no need for him to leave immediately, he would be delighted to take Miss Thomason back in his carriage later in the day. Stephen offered with alacrity to escort Hermione and the two of them left almost immediately before Rachel could protest,

Stephen once again riding alongside Hermione's carriage as he had but two days earlier.

The day was another fine one and Amelia soon brought down to her uncle messages from both Persephone and Mr. Ramsey inquiring as to whether there was any way that they could be carried out into the garden. As the stairs of The Green Man were unusually wide, and as Mr. Tewks was more than willing to help, the transfer was soon managed, and the invalids found themselves seated side by side, each with a leg supported by numerous cushions, in comfortable armchairs in the garden. Rachel and Hezekiah disappeared almost immediately, intent, they said, upon exploring further the neighborhood in which they seemed likely to be spending considerable time, and Amelia offered to read to the invalids, since both appeared still to be a bit fretful. She asked what they might prefer, offering the wide variety of novels and poetry that Rachel and Hermione had brought, but as each appeared determined to defer to the other with a politeness which Amelia found excruciating, she eventually settled on one of the volumes which *she* had never read, Mr Scott's *Rob Roy.* The choice was an unfortunate one Persephone had no taste for Scott's adventures, and Mr. Ramsey had read the work when it first appeared some years earlier. Neither, however, raised an objection, and Amelia happily set to reading, unaware that each of her listeners was entirely lost in thought, hearing scarcely so much as a word. Thus the morning passed, with Persephone and Ramsey each deep in a blue funk, Amelia deep in her novel, and Hezekiah and Rachel deep in the nearby woods.

As the time approached for luncheon, Rachel reappeared, informing the rest that Mr. Arrington had wandered off but should be back shortly to take his meal before leaving for the City. She would, she said, go with him, and did not expect to return for several days, one of her maternal aunts was arriving in London that very day and she could not in all politeness abandon the lady on her first days in Town. She and Amelia then retired together to the kitchen to request food, leaving Persephone and Ramsey once again to each other's company, bound as they were to their chairs. They passed the time unprofitably, silently glaring at each other until the entire party reassembled for a picnic lunch in the garden, served by the ever-willing Molly with the (to his master) unexpected assistance of Mr. Ramsey's valet.

Luncheon complete, Hezekiah and Rachel took their leave, and Amelia prepared to resume her reading. Persephone, however, had had quite enough, and told Amelia that she might, perhaps, prefer some other form of diversion. Amelia was more than willing to oblige but in fact the options open to them were few, and when Persephone said wistfully that she wished her uncle had been able to stay the afternoon, so that he could have diverted her with more chess, Ramsey spoke up.

"I don't think I'm up to your uncle's class, but if you wish, *we* might play." Ramsey's motives in making the offer were simple; he was bored to distraction, and whatever else might be said of Persephone Welton, it was clear that she *would* provide him with an interesting game of chess. Persephone, no less bored, agreed, silently vowing to *annihilate* the insufferable man.

In point of fact, the game was a very close one, although Persephone did, in the end, manage a victory. Ramsey's game lacked his opponent's dash, but was nonetheless quite solid, and Persephone repeatedly found herself in difficulties which she had not foreseen. Inevitably, they talked as the game progressed, Ramsey inquiring in a conciliatory tone how it came about that Mrs. Welton was so very addicted to a game that many women find tedious, and Persephone amusing him with a few tales both of her eccentric governess and her eccentric friend, Anna Milbanke. Her stories about Anna led almost inevitably to a discussion of Lord Byron for whom they found they shared a grudging admiration, Ramsey for his command of meter (something about which Persephone had no opinion), and Persephone for his sheer daring and flair. Their conversation was guarded, both carefully avoiding any statements to which the other could take offense, but there is no denying that by the time the game was done, they were in more charity with each other than they had been. They were also, however, each quite tired. Calling once again on the good-natured landlord, then, Amelia assisted both up to their rooms and left them sleeping soundly for the balance of the afternoon. Amelia, who'd paid attention neither to the game nor to the conversation which accompanied it, returned to the garden to continue her daydreams and her perusal of *Rob Roy* and silence reigned.

Not so in London. Stephen had enjoyed a delightful ride back to the city with Hermione, who confessed to him that her story about an engagement had been untrue. "In fact," she'd said, with a bewitching smile, "I had no desire in the *first place* to visit my uncle again, and I only came because Rachel *insisted,* and because I hoped that I might see *you.*" Once it became clear, she went on, that *he* would not remain at the inn, she was determined that neither should *she,* and had acted accordingly. She had *hoped* that he would arrange somehow to act as her escort, but had never *dreamed* that everything would work out so wonderfully well, with Rachel remaining behind. While Rachel would, doubtless, be back sometime during the early part of the afternoon, they had the whole morning to do what they wished! There were so many places to which Hermione had never been, and to which she feared that Uncle Peter would not take her, and could *Stephen* possibly? Stephen, besotted, agreed readily, though he blanched a bit when he heard that where Hermione wished to go was a fair that had been set up recently on the outskirts of the City. He ventured to suggest that she might find the crowd a bit boisterous, but Hermione waved aside these objections with a flick of her dainty hand, and leaned up to tell the coachman to drive straight to the fair.

Upon their arrival, Stephen saw all of his worst fears confirmed. The crowd was large, noisy, and exceedingly vulgar, and he attempted to convince Hermione, now that she had seen what it looked like, to come away. Hermione, however, was not to be convinced. Apostrophizing Stephen as nearly as dull as Uncle Peter, Hermione jumped down lightly from the carriage, leaving Stephen no choice but to hand his horse to the coachman and follow.

The next few hours had, for Stephen, a nightmare quality that he would remember for the rest of his life. Hermione was set upon extracting the maximum enjoyment from this stolen adventure, and was continually dashing off in new directions. He could scarcely keep up with her, but discovered shortly that his attention was, of necessity, divided between the lady and the steady stream of men who posed some threat to her. Thus, before they had been at the fair for fifteen minutes, Stephen had interrupted no fewer than three attempts to cut Hermione's reticule off her wrist. Another half-hour had not gone by when a burly young farmer had to be dissuaded from carrying her off to the House of Horrors, a dark tent from which issued the sound of women's squeals, not all of them fearful. Most of the (many) comments thrown their way were, fortunately, incomprehensible to Hermione (and sometimes to Stephen as well), but they made it obvious that the fashionable Beauty was of nearly as much interest to the crowd as the various freaks.

Through all of this, his lordship maintained a steady pleading that they leave before some trouble occurred, but Hermione steadfastly refused. He was, she was certain, making too much of the attention they were receiving; some of the young men *might* appear overly attentive, but she was quite accustomed to that, and was sure that they meant no harm. In any event, there were still *dozens* of things that she wanted to see, and she was not about to be thwarted *again.* She promised to hold on to her reticule *very* tightly, and informed Stephen that if he didn't want strangers to take her to the House of Horrors, he should do so himself. This he was unwilling to do, but he did reluctantly agree to purchase tickets for the melodrama that was to begin in few minutes. Although he was certain that it would contain some matters inappropriate for Hermione, he thought that, on balance, they would be better off sitting in one place where they would not be so conspicuous and where he might more easily keep his eye upon her.

In the event, the play was so warm that Stephen found himself blushing. This was certainly not the sort of entertainment to which he was accustomed to bring a lady; he would have hesitated to take a bit of muslin here. And Hermione seemed to enjoy it! It was apparent that she simply did not understand the more dubious passages, but what she did comprehend was bad enough. Stephen prided himself on his sophistication and experience; indeed, in Society he affected rather a cynical and world-weary pose. Further, his formative years had been spent with a singularly strong-minded sister who had given him little taste for mere missishness. Still, Hermione's behavior left him profoundly shocked. He was accustomed to independence, and prepared for willfulness; he was unused to simple vulgarity. By the time the play was complete, he was determined to get Hermione out of the fair, if he had to throw her over his shoulder to do it, and he was giving serious thought, for the first time, to Miss Thomason's and Ramsey's appraisals of her character. Hermione had her charms, no doubt, but there was also some truth in the others' condemnations of her. He could not for a moment imagine either his sister or his cousin disporting themselves in this fashion, and while he was willing to give full credit to the shortcomings of extreme youth, he began to wonder whether he should not have shown more sympathy toward Peter Ramsey.

Thus, upon leaving the tent in which the play had been presented, Stephen took Hermione's arm in a firm grip, intent on preventing her from charging off in a new direction. As this was precisely her plan, she received something of a shock when her headlong rush was checked and turned to him in amazement. Indeed, so amazed was she that it was some time before she could be brought to understand that Stephen was serious about extricating her from the fair. As soon as she did understand it, however, her nostrils flared, her small mouth grew set, and her eyes took on a stormy cast.

Initially, at least, her voice was low. "Take your hand off of me this *instant,* Stephen Arrington. *You're* not my uncle, to be ordering me about and dragging me off as if I were a *schoolgirl*! You said you would take me where I wished to go, and I wish to remain here!"

Stephen was attempting to keep a sharp hold on his temper, and answered in a calm enough voice. "Really, Hermione, you must be reasonable. I'll take you anywhere a lady of fashion should be, but this place is outside of enough. I shudder to think what your uncle would say if he had had the privilege of viewing the entertainment *we* just saw, and what is worse, everything he would say would be quite true! Surely you must perceive that we are attracting an undesirable amount of attention, and that cannot be acceptable to you, while as for the exhibits, they are dreadfully common." He smiled and added, in much the tone he would have adopted toward a fractious child, "Come away now, and I promise that I'll think of some more amusing diversion."

Hermione appeared to hear none of this speech; her uncle or Rachel could have warned Stephen that she was, in fact, rapidly working herself up into a tantrum during which she was likely to become both impervious to reason and oblivious to her surroundings. Her small frame increasingly rigid and her mouth increasingly set, she simply glared at Stephen for a moment, and then said in a voice that began in a whisper and ended in a shout, "*Everyone* conspires to thwart me, even *you.* Whenever there is something *I* want to do, it isn't 'proper for a lady' or 'the sort of thing a lady would enjoy.' Well, I *do* enjoy it, and I *won't* be bullied, and I *will* stay here and you *will* TAKE YOUR HAND OFF MY ARM!"

At that, Hermione burst into a storm of tears, while Stephen stared, aghast. He thought wildly that he had been mistaken earlier when he believed that they were attracting an unfortunate amount of attention; he had not known then what the attention of a crowd could be. One had gathered around them almost as soon as Hermione began her speech, and by the finish, a heated debate was raging, with the women by and large taking the view that a girl should listen to her man (particularly when he's such a handsome one), and the men largely urging Stephen either to let the little thing have her way, or to let some man who knew how to handle a woman step in. Hermione appeared to hear none of this, simply continuing to rage at Stephen while he tried to lead her through the thickening mob. He almost shouted with relief when he spied John Coachman, hoping that the man could at least help to open up a path for them. In fact, however, he did something considerably more direct. Pausing simply to inform Stephen that he had seen Miss in this state before, and that there was no purpose to be served by talking to her as she would pay attention to nothing that was said or done, he unceremoniously picked her up, and as Stephen had considered doing earlier, carried her off over his shoulder, leaving Stephen to cover their retreat and to ward off the numerous men who volunteered, depending on their moods, to relieve John of his fair burden or to mill him down and rescue the damsel.

By the time they reached the coach, Hermione's sobs had subsided and the crowd had thinned. Stephen had not had to knock anyone down, although he had been compelled to push some aside with more force than finesse. He was tired and tousled and was trying extremely hard to resist the temptation to take Hermione over his knee and spank her. To think that he had actually fancied himself in love with the chit! It was enough to make his blood run cold. Thanking John profusely for having come to his rescue, he ordered him to drive the carriage home and mounted his own horse. He felt constrained to accompany Hermione to the Ramsey residence, but after consigning her to the care of the housekeeper, and without exchanging so much as another word with her, he had returned, at last, to his own lodgings. By the time Rachel reached Town in the late afternoon, Hermione had recovered herself and had bribed John handsomely to keep his story to himself, and as Stephen chose never to repeat the tale, it remained a secret. Persephone was relieved, however, to find that when she next saw Stephen, he appeared to have recovered entirely from his brief infatuation; when asked if he had enjoyed accompanying Miss Pendergast back to Town, he had yawned, and remarked that very *young* ladies could be a bit tedious, couldn't they?

Fifteen

The next morning brought Amelia a message from her father announcing that he would be forced to remain in Town for a few days, as matters had arisen which required his personal attention. Lest Amelia worry, his note ended with a bitter animadversion on the incompetence of assistants who were unable so much as to tie their own cravats without their employer looking over their shoulder. As the morning also brought Stephen (and not Hermione) to The Green Man, Amelia could not pretend to be vastly disappointed at her parent's absence, and after Persephone found a moment to pass on to her Stephen's surprising comment about Hermione, Amelia virtually glowed. Both Persephone and Ramsey, on the other hand, regarded Hezekiah's absence as a disadvantage, as both had relied on him to divert them. They spent the morning in their respective rooms reading, and by luncheon were thoroughly tired of their own company. Each ate a solitary meal off of a tray in bed and looked forward with no small degree of trepidation to the remaining period of convalescence, trying to imagine how they would survive the wearisome weeks. Dr. Traherne stopped in briefly in the early afternoon and pronounced each to be doing well, but was able to hold out no hope for an early return to Town. When Amelia and Stephen stopped in to see Persephone after the doctor had left, they found her looking glum.

Stephen pinched his sister's chin lightly, and said sympathetically, "Blue as a megrim, ain't you, Perse? Can't say that I blame you; this room is well enough to sleep in, but I wouldn't fancy spending the whole day here myself."

"A whole *day* would be little enough problem, Stephen, but how am I to spend whole *weeks?* I suppose I shall be driven to fancy sewing, and you know how I *hate* to sew."

"Well, you won't, you know, because I have a much more clever idea. The weather is still holding up remarkably fine, and I think that if the mammoth Tewks and I put our heads (or, at least, my head and his back) together, we could rig a very nice little shelter to allow you to sit in the garden and be shielded from the wind, which is the only thing that makes sittin' still right now a little ineligible. And I've brought Amelia's painting things from Town, and we could set up an easel for you, and you two could paint together, and I could read to you both, and it would be as jolly as jolly can possibly be."

At this point, Ramsey's voice could be heard from the next room, asking plaintively if Stephen had any intention of including *him* in these plans? He might not like the Arringtons, but they were the only company he was likely to have for the next weeks, and he had no intention of spending his time a virtual prisoner in his room simply to avoid *them.*

Having received, then, enthusiastic support for his plan from both of the invalids, Stephen went to seek out Mr. Tewks and present it to him. Tewks, ever willing to perform any task that took him out of the inn and out from under his wife's eye, agreed with an equal degree of enthusiasm, and the work soon commenced, with Stephen returning periodically upstairs to report on its progress. Amelia, intending at first simply to spend the afternoon with Persephone, took pity on Mr. Ramsey and suggested to Stephen that he could carry his sister into Ramsey's room so that the latter would not spend the day alone. Ramsey and Persephone, remembering their very sound reasons for wishing a truce to reign between them at least for the duration of their stay at The Green Man, each agreed, and Persephone's transfer was accomplished in minutes. However, when Amelia offered to resume her reading of *Rob Roy* aloud, they both protested, laughingly confessing their separate objections. Persephone's, though, that she simply had no use for Mr. Scott sparked a literary dispute that raged for the next several hours, as each of the three attempted to convince the others that, respectively, novels (Ramsey), poetry (Amelia), and essays (Persephone) were the only things worth reading. The dispute was marked equally by its wide range and its good nature, and by the time Stephen reappeared in the late afternoon with the announcement that by the next morning, they would no longer be confined inside, he found the three talking and laughing like old friends. Informed of what he had missed, he professed himself profoundly grateful as he would only have embarrassed himself among three such bluestockings, but when commanded to settle the argument for good and all, he sided with Amelia, claiming that Perse's essays gave him headaches, and Ramsey's novels, gas.

On that note, and after returning his sister to her room, Stephen carried Amelia off to dinner and if that meal was not quite so informal as their first together at the inn, neither was it so subdued as those they had taken in Hezekiah's company. As the moon was full, Stephen determined to ride back to London as soon as their meal was complete, and Amelia and Persephone passed a pleasant evening in Persephone's room, chatting and reading. That some of their conversation revolved on the surprising turn their discussion with Mr. Ramsey had taken that afternoon was to be expected; that Persephone found herself unwillingly conceding that the man was, perhaps, not quite so insufferable as he had at first seemed was not. Amelia used the opportunity to ask her cousin exactly why it was that she had taken Mr. Ramsey in such aversion, confessing that she herself was favorably impressed by the man.

Persephone had given some thought to the question of whether she would enlighten her cousin concerning Mr. Ramsey's offer to her. On balance, she decided that it would not be fair; the man's behavior might have been abominable, but he was not entirely without excuse, and to reveal it to Amelia would simply turn her against him. After some hesitation, then, she had answered, "The story is not a pretty one, although I'm no longer convinced that Mr. Ramsey is very much to blame. You must know that I was disposed against him as soon as I heard that he had been an intimate of Captain Welton. I've not told you very much about my husband; I see no good reason to speak ill of the dead. But believe me when I tell you that a former friendship with David Welton is *not* a recommendation of a man's character." Seeing an odd expression on her cousin's face, she went on, "I can see that I've shocked you, and indeed these are hard things for a wife to say of a husband not one year dead."

Here, Amelia interrupted. "No. You misunderstand me. I'm not shocked *at* you, but only *for* you. I'd no idea that you'd been that unhappy with Captain Welton. I knew, of course, that your marriage was not a fortuitous one, but I've never really known the reasons, other than the fact that you had little money. I believe that I can think of few sadder fates than finding oneself married to a man you could not respect." At this, Amelia seemed to sink into thought, and Persephone continued, telling her cousin the story of the late Captain Welton's iniquities, as recounted to her by Mr. Ramsey. She concluded, "I'm afraid that my reaction to Mr. Ramsey was much like that which certain Greeks are said to have had to messengers of ill-tidings; I blamed him for the wrong which he simply recounted." Then, remembering the scene at Almack's, she suddenly laughed. "Do you remember the morning before the accident, when you commented that you had noticed a broken vase at Almack's and couldn't think how it had come to be so badly smashed, and I told you that I thought a wind must have taken it? I'm very much ashamed to confess that *I* was that wind." And at that, both women burst out laughing.

Ramsey, hearing them from his bed, smiled as well. He had taken quite a fancy to Amelia Arrington, who reminded him strongly of her late mother. (In point of fact, Mrs. Arrington had been no more handsome than her daughter was, but neither her dusky skin nor the fact that she was married to Hezekiah had kept a youthful Ramsey from falling secretly but desperately in love with her for a time.) As for the widow, their debate of that afternoon had completed the work which their chess game had already begun of convincing him that he had seriously misjudged the woman. How it came about that David Welton had wooed and won a lady not only of extraordinary beauty but of intelligence and refinement would remain a mystery; that he had, in fact, done so was now obvious. Ramsey was pleased, then, to hear that Mrs. Welton's spirits appeared to be improving, and pleased also to think that his convalescence might not be so grim as he had at first feared. Sandston, showing unexpected good will, had taken back with him a list of books that Ramsey fancied he might enjoy, and Ramsey was, therefore, looking forward to the prospect of days spent in the out-of-doors in pleasant company and evenings passed with amusing authors. Like Persephone, then, Ramsey ended the day in quite a cheerful state of mind.

During the next weeks, the inhabitants of The Green Man settled down into a comfortable routine. Hezekiah had returned from Town with the news that he would not, as he had hoped, be able to take up full-time residence at The Green Man for the remaining period of his niece's stay there; certain matters relating to trade had been raised in Parliament, and his presence was imperative. He promised to come out regularly and did so, and even his daughter confessed to her cousins that his occasional absence was not, perhaps, such a very bad thing.

Each morning, Persephone, Amelia, and Ramsey breakfasted in their own rooms, attended by their own servants, and enjoying a lazy and leisurely meal ranging in size from Amelia's cup of chocolate and a single sweet biscuit to Ramsey's full array of sirloin, kippers, eggs, and ale. By midmorning, Stephen would arrive, bearing the latest *on dits* and scandals, including the rumors which were beginning to rock London that the king, newly crowned, was intending to bring a formal bill of divorcement against Queen Caroline in the House of Lords. In deference to Ramsey's comparatively lonely state, Stephen would generally visit him first with the news, and even made a point of bringing information about political and business matters in which he took no interest so that Ramsey would not feel too cut off. After speaking to Ramsey for a half-hour or so, Stephen would retire to Persephone's room, pass on to her whatever he thought would amuse *her,* and then would hunt out the landlord for assistance in getting Ramsey downstairs.

While Stephen was busy with the invalids, Amelia would go out to the garden to set up her easel. At the urging of Stephen and Persephone, she was doing a rather ambitious series of studies of the environs of the inn, and was still involved in preliminary sketches of all the views that could be had from the area of the garden. After Persephone and Ramsey saw Amelia's work, each indicated an interest in drawing under her tutelage, as did Stephen, so the latter part of the mornings was passed in what became a communal art lesson, with all four drawing whatever view Amelia chose, and Amelia (reluctantly, and only after the others had insisted) critiquing their work. Lunch was, more often than not, a picnic in the garden, served by Molly and George who had, their masters had been informed, reached "an understanding," by which it was meant that George understood that he wasn't going to get anywhere with Molly unless he married her, and Molly understood that she was, at last, going to live in the metropolis.

After lunch, Stephen and Amelia would generally wander off to view some more distant prospect than could be seen from the garden, and George would set up the chess board on a deal table between Persephone and Ramsey. Their daily games were a great pleasure to each, as it transpired that they were, in fact, well matched. By the time a few days had passed, all restraint between them had broken down, as each confessed him or herself to have been much in the wrong. Indeed, Ramsey was so magnanimous as to admit that he had grossly mishandled his horse and grossly misjudged not only Mrs. Welton herself but brother as well, whom he now described as a bit of a rattle, but also a true gentleman. Persephone admitted in turn that at least part of the reason for her rage at his comments about her family had been her sense that there was some truth in his words; certainly, her father had been a sad rake and, if not quite a complete fribble, certainly not the most *stable* of individuals.

After thus clearing the air between them, Ramsey

and Persephone discovered that they rubbed along remarkably well together, sharing many tastes and interests, and even sharing that most elusive of qualities, the ability to enjoy a restful silence. Indeed, Ramsey was surprised to discover that Persephone's dramatic appearance was misleading; perhaps her most dominant characteristic was her tranquility, hard won over the years of coping with her far-from-tranquil relatives. Remembering his earlier expectations that the widow of David Welton must certainly be a Dasher, he was ncreasingly taken aback to discover, instead, a somewhat quiet woman of an almost bluestocking bent, with a dry sense of humor and an ineffable quality of, well, Quality.

Persephone, in her turn, found Ramsey to be a welcome relief from most of the men whom she had known, including her late husband and even her beloved brother. Recalling Welton, and comparing him with Ramsey, she wondered that she had ever believed herself in love with so *trivial* a man. That Welton had turned out to be a rake, a gambler, and a wastrel was, perhaps, more than she could have foreseen, but she had known him to be interested in little more than horses, routs, and mills even before she married him, nd had believed that it didn't signify. A grand romanic passion had seemed enough; it had never occurred o her that she might wish to be able to *converse* with er husband. Now, after spending many hours each ay with a man whose interests ranged from political o artistic, she could not believe that she had once been o easily contented.

And so the days passed in considerable harmony. Persephone watched with some interest the progress of he friendship between her cousin and her brother. She had long since penetrated Amelia's secret, and had at rst believed with considerable sorrow that her case as hopeless. Now, however, she was not so sure. Stephen's attitude toward his cousin certainly appeared to partake of little of the lover; he treated her with an easy camaraderie that was still reminiscent of his behavior toward his sister. Still, he continued to dance attendance long after it was apparent that his sister did not need his attentions and Persephone noticed that he appeared as eager as Amelia for the times when the two of them would wander off together, and that he looked singularly contented when they returned from these outings. If he had, indeed, fallen in love with Amelia, he was for once keeping his own counsel but that, his sister thought, was not necessarily a bad thing. If forced to be honest, she would have confessed that she herself was doing much the same thing, and was inclined to think that it might be the very sincerity of his emotion which tied his tongue. In any event, she believed now that some sort of understanding might well be reached between the two, and as she had grown even more fond of her cousin after coming to know her better, she hoped that she was correct. As to her own situation, she was also content for the time being to sit back, figuratively as she was forced to do literally and see what time would bring, time being the one thing of which she and Mr. Ramsey had, for the moment, a surfeit.

Of Hermione, little had been seen in the weeks following the accident. Rachel returned every few days to check on the progress of her friend and of Mr. Ramsey. Like Stephen, she brought small bits of news that she had treasured up for the invalids. However, Hermione only rarely accompanied her, and while Rachel attempted to reassure Ramsey that the girl was behaving herself with reasonable decorum, Ramsey confided t Persephone that he believed that she was probably slipping the halter behind Rachel's back now that he wa no longer there to back her authority with his own. H seemed philosophical about this, admitting with a sig that he had nearly run out of ideas for controlling hi ward in any event and hoping that the worst follies she would commit would be *private* ones. As it turned out, even this modest wish was not to be fulfilled.

It was approaching the end of the fourth week after he accident. Dr. Traherne, who had checked his paients regularly, came by early one morning and proounced the two fit to be moved; indeed, he brought with him a pair of crutches for Persephone with which, e said, she might begin to practice getting around, so ong as she did not try to go too far. Ramsey, he said, vould be ready to follow shortly.

After a brief and triumphant trip around her room, Persephone felt herself to be exhausted. Suggesting wistfully that it might be nice to spend one last day in he garden, she and Ramsey were carried out one last me to their shelter, the chess board set between them. They were chatting in a desultory fashion as they set p the pieces, when they heard the sound of Hezekiah's oice in the inn, asking in an agitated tone where Mr. amsey was to be found. With Rachel by his side, he vas shown out to the garden by Molly. Waiting only or the girl to return to the inn, Rachel had burst out, Mr. Ramsey, I am so very, very sorry, but I have the ost appalling news; Hermione has eloped with reddy Harris!"

Before Ramsey could respond, Hezekiah broke in. Hmph. Don't like to say it, but feel responsible. Been king Rachel away from her duties. Fact is, married er. Yesterday. Special license." And with that, he took s wife's hand and raised his chin defiantly, looking, ersephone thought, a great deal like a pugnacious hoolboy.

The stunned silence that followed was broken at last a shout of delighted laughter from Ramsey, laughter which, after a few moments, they all joined. When could catch his breath, Ramsey held his hand out Hezekiah and told him that he admired his judgment, envied his happiness, and wished him nothing but the best in the world. Still laughing, he turned to Rachel then and said, "Mrs. Arrington, I could not be more pleased to find that at least *some* good has come of that little devil's descent upon the London scene. I can only be grateful that my condition deters any thought of my chasing after the happy couple to prevent nuptials which I firmly believe are the best thing that could happen to my misbegotten niece. Harris, though hardly a man whom I would choose for a sensible woman, is not near so bad a match as Hermione might have made; at the least, he is neither a fortune hunter nor a rake, and if he is such a fool as to have married the girl, thank the Lord that is his problem and not mine. My only question is why they ran away? I would have been perfectly contented to bless the match."

Rachel had an answer for this. "My good sir, you have surely forgotten your niece's unrivaled talent for drama. You must believe that Hermione painted such a dark picture of your tyranny over her that the poor Mr. Harris actually believed that an elopement was necessary. I'm sure that the poor boy is, even now, cowering in some country inn, awaiting your descent as an avenging angel!"

"You're right, of course. I almost hate to disappoint the boy. Nonetheless, I feel I must." And with that, he deputized Rachel (and her bridegroom) to take such measures as they could to discover where the newlyweds had gone and to send them word that it was safe for them to return to London. The Arringtons agreed willingly, and added that they should attempt to cover up the fact of the elopement by such announcements and such pretense of family joy as was possible.

While Persephone was joining her felicitations to those of Ramsey, Amelia and Stephen wandered up, drawn by the sound of voices. They heard with som amazement the announcement of Hezekiah and Rachel's union and of Hermione's, though Stephen contended that this was exactly what might have been anticipated. While Persephone was explaining the situation, Amelia appeared to take great interest in the toes of her sandals, while Stephen watched her with a pronounced smile. After Persephone finished, Stephen took a deep breath. He then stepped up to his uncle and, after congratulating him on his own good fortune, pointedly requested a private audience at his earliest possible convenience. Hezekiah looked from his nephew to his blushing daughter, nodded grimly, and invited Stephen to step into the parlor of the inn. While they were gone, Amelia confessed what was obvious to all, that she and Stephen had determined to make a match of it. She received their congratulations, but continued to look nervously toward the parlor until Rachel claimed the right of a mama-in-law to reassure her new daughter; laughingly, she told Amelia that she and Hezekiah had already discussed the obvious attachment of the cousins, and that she had persuaded him to give not only his approval, but his wholehearted blessing. Hezekiah, she said, had come to value Stephen most highly in recent weeks and if he still could find it in his heart to wish Stephen were somewhat more serious and steady, he was ready to believe that sincere love would do him wonders. When Hezekiah poked his head out the inn's back door to summon his bride and daughter inside, then, Amelia was ready to obey the summons with a cheerful smile and a light step.

Thus, Ramsey and Persephone found themselves once again alone. Ramsey continued where he had left off in setting up the chess pieces, while Persephone silently studied her hands. After a few moments, Ramsey said in a meditative tone of voice, "We do seem to be the only two left, don't we?"

Persephone, her tone matching his, agreed. "Personally, I've often observed love to be a contagious ailment; when Stephen and I were barely more than children, we were *always* in love at the same time. I think it gets into the air."

"In love often, were you?"

"Constantly, I believe."

"Any time recently?"

"Mmm."

"Anyone I know?"

"Mmm."

"Persephone Welton. Damn my leg, and damn this chair, and damn my blighted horse, but I'll have you know that *I* was one of the idiots who took your husband's wagers, and if you *won't* marry me, it would be little worse than a cheat! Welton may have been a scoundrel, but he was exceedingly punctilious about matters of play, and he will never rest easy in his grave unless you redeem his vowel!"

"Mr. Ramsey, are you asking me to marry you to redeem my late husband's honor as a gamester?"

"That, and the fact that I can't stand the idea of being without you. Persephone, my love, *will* you marry me?"

Persephone looked at Ramsey, suddenly serious, and nodded her head slightly. "Of course I will. How else could I save you the next time you decide to ride a horse you can't handle?"

A few minutes later, Mrs. Tewks wandered out to the garden to discover when luncheon should be needed. She had heard Dr. Traherne's pronouncement, and now that she was about to lose her unwelcome party, she realized that she would be sorry to see them go. Their influence on Tewks had been, of course, of the very worst, while she viewed the loss of Molly in the light of a personal insult. Still, the injured lady and gentleman had turned out to be most pleasant, as had their various friends and relations, and there was no denying that she was considerably plumper in the pocket than she had expected to be this early in the year. Being of a saving disposition, this weighed heavily with her, and she decided to put out a handsome spread to commemorate her guests' final day under her roof. The sight that met her eyes was, however, a shocking one. There was Mrs. Welton, her crutches discarded on the grass beside Mr. Ramsey's chair, perched precariously on the gentleman's one good leg and, apparently, tickling his ear with one of her own long curls. She turned from this abandoned prospect, only to find Miss Arrington and his lordship lost in an embrace in the parlor, while in the kitchen, George and Molly could be heard making plans for their own wedding. Looking out the window, she spied Miss Thomason and the nabob arm in arm, smiling foolishly at each other and strolling off toward the woods.

"Lord a' mercy," she exclaimed, and then smiled. "Where's Tewks?"